Sophie
and the
Rising Sun

Augusta Trobaugh

A *Time Warner* Paperback

First published in Great Britain in 2002
by Little, Brown
This edition published by Time Warner Paperbacks in 2003

A CIP catalogue record for this book
is available from the British Library.

ISBN 0 7515 3245 2

Typeset in Perpetua by M Rules
Printed and bound in Great Britain by
Clays Ltd, St Ives plc

Time Warner Paperbacks
An imprint of
Time Warner Books UK
Brettenham House
Lancaster Place
London WC2E 7EN

www.TimeWarnerBooks.co.uk

For my daughter, Melanie,

a true romantic

Sophie
and the
Rising Sun

Chapter One

*M*iss Anne said:

Some folks in this town still think I know what really happened to Sophie—leastwise those folks old enough to remember Pearl Harbor and the terrible days that followed.

Why, to this very day—over twenty years later— once in a while, somebody will say to me, "Miss Anne, you can tell me what *really* happened to Sophie, now that it's been so long."

But I can't tell them.

Because I was never sure.

And I guess the reason they ask in the first place is that most of us still care about Sophie and want to know that she's all right.

To be truthful, I guess everybody in town—leastwise those old enough to remember—always felt a little bit bad for Sophie, how she wasted all her youth and beauty—and to be perfectly truthful, there was precious little of the latter—taking care of her mama and those two old aunts. Everybody used to say that one day, Sophie would just up and run off and get married. When she was younger, I mean. But she never did. Guess you have to have a young man to do something like that, and I don't think there was anyone who was interested in her.

There was a little talk about a beau, just before the Great War—World War One—but most of those boys never came home again. Boyd and Andrew and Henry and others whose names I can't remember now, so if there was ever someone who was interested in Sophie— and I doubt it—he must have been one of them. It really didn't matter, anyway, because if anyone had come around about Sophie, her mama and the aunts would have nipped that right in the bud. I'm sure of it.

"Nothing lasts," her mama used to say. "So no use in Sophie getting started with it."

Sophie's mama was always like that. Bitter, in general. And about men, in particular. How on earth she ever agreed to marry any man is beyond me. All I can say is that Mr. Willis must have slipped her some elderberry wine or something. Because they only kept company for about a month or so, and the whole time, everybody in town could hear her berating him in a loud voice, right there on her front porch when he came courting. But he just kept on coming. Sat right there in the swing and smiled off into space while she went into tirade after tirade. Maybe she finally wore herself out.

Mr. Willis was quite elderly, and I guess he'd learned plenty of patience. Of course, Sophie's mama was certainly no spring chicken herself, by then, but she hadn't learned anything about patience. Never did, to tell the truth. But I guess one thing that kept Mr. Willis coming around was that he figured it was his last chance to get married.

So—somehow or other—he got her to the church.

Then he took her off on a grand honeymoon trip to New Orleans for two whole weeks, and when he brought her back, she was with child—we found out later. Only about a week after that, Mr. Willis died in his sleep. Left her a well-off widow with a nice, big house. And he left her Sophie, too, though she didn't realize that right away. And of course, that was certainly some surprise when she found that out. She sent right off to Atlanta for her two old maid sisters—Elsa and Minnie—to come and live with her. And they did.

But goodness, what a time they had of it, especially right at first. Because Sophie's mama must have thought that *they* were going to wait on her hand and foot, and those older sisters must have thought the same thing about *her* waiting on them. Led to an awful lot of fussing and pouting, it did. But eventually, they learned how to get along right well, I guess.

And of course, they were happy about the baby that was coming, so that settled them down a bit. Almost every single evening for months, you could see them sitting together on the porch, crocheting to beat the band—with their heads down and their crochet needles just flashing away. Went at it with a vengeance, they did. Why, by the time that baby was ready to come, they had enough clothes for a whole army of babies! Caps and sacques and booties and sweaters and blankets. But of course, not a single one of them could crochet worth a flip, so the sweaters all had one long sleeve and one short, and the caps would have fit a watermelon, they were so big. And the blankets came out shaped like triangles, for the most part. Still, they did their best, and I guess their hearts were in the right place.

Well, the baby started coming on a Thursday morning—and it turned out to be the longest labor in the history of Salty Creek. By Friday night, everybody in town could hear the screaming, and around noon on Saturday, she was shrieking, "Shoot me! For God's sake, somebody shoot me!"

I was hardly more than a child myself. Only twelve or thirteen, and my mama made me stay in the back part of our house so I wouldn't hear any more than she could help. Wouldn't even let me sit out on the porch.

The doctor came and went at their house until Saturday afternoon, and after that, he never left until the baby finally arrived, around church-time on Sunday. Folks said that when he came out about an hour later, he looked like he'd been run over by a train, he did. Went straight home, his wife said, drank a fifth of bourbon, and slept for two whole days. Later, he told her he'd never seen anything like it. Just flat out a little baby that didn't want to be born. "I had to drag it out!" he said. "And God only knows what-all it was hanging on to!"

Sophie's mama always said the birth ruined her health. And I guess all the hand-wringing and the hollering and the running into each other the elder sisters did must have taken a toll, too. Because they said the birth ruined *their* health as well. So that as soon as Sophie could toddle around and understand when they told her to go get their crocheting for them or another pillow to rest their feet on, or a clean hanky, they had her doing everything for them. All the time. Just like she owed them something.

It must have been hard for Sophie, waiting on them hand and foot from the time she was just a little thing. And growing up under the black little bird-eyes of those women. And none of them young. In a house full of medicine bottles and handkerchiefs and smelling salts. And boredom.

That's why I say that if there was ever a beau for Sophie, they would have nipped that right in the bud. Because they weren't about to give up the one who ran around and waited on them. Besides, Sophie would have told me if there had been someone. I'm sure of it.

So she never did marry. Just took care of those old ladies and grew older and more faded-looking herself, every single year, what with them getting so elderly and so much more demanding and living for such a long time. And Sophie's mama, especially, was always hard to get along with. When she got older, she took to doing some strange things, like collecting dead birds she'd find out in the yard from time to time. Take them right inside the house and lay them out on a shelf in the pantry. Such as that.

She was the first one to pass on, Sophie's mama was, and I always thought somebody ought to have put her on a shelf in the pantry, too—let her see how she liked having that done to her. But of course, they didn't. Then a few years later, Sophie's Aunt Elsa passed on. Her Aunt Minnie was the only one left after that, and she was just as senile as a coot for a long time before she finally passed away. Used to sneak out of the house almost every night and wander around in the front yard in her nightgown, calling and calling for her mama. Can you imagine? Sophie never had a whole night's sleep for all the years that went on, but she didn't complain about it. Not even to me.

Afterward, when they were all gone at last—her Aunt Minnie passing on only a few months after Mr. Oto came to stay in my gardener's cottage—folks thought then maybe Sophie would do a little traveling or something like that. But she didn't. Just went about doing what she'd always done—taking care of the house and tending to her crab traps and painting some pictures down by the river. I guess by then it was too late for much of anything else.

But I'll say this about Sophie: She was a real lady. One of the few left in this whole town, someone who was raised right—whatever other faults her mama and the aunts may have had. So Sophie always came calling on me—and she was the only one who still kept up that fine old tradition.

I was a little bit older, of course, and I'd known Sophie all her life, knew her better than is usual in small towns like this one, where everybody knows everybody else, anyway. Because when I was a young lady—and already being courted by my late husband—Sophie was just a little girl, and even then, I thought she was very special.

Maybe it had something to do with the way I'd always wanted a sister. Someone younger than me to look up to me and share her little secrets with me. Sophie was the closest I had to that. But of course, her mama didn't let her get away very often, so it didn't blossom into the real friendship—like sisters—it could have been. Still, I always thought she was a precious little thing.

I remember one twilight evening when I was sitting in the porch swing, and Sophie came skipping down the road right in front of my house—she couldn't have been more than six or seven—and waved her fingers at me as she went by. Must have gotten away from her mama for a few minutes. She was wearing a white pinafore and skipping and singing right down the middle of the road, and I thought she looked so pretty that day. And, too, there was something about the way it was, right at dusk, that made me think she looked just like a little white egret, ruffling its feathers this way and that. But if her mama had seen her, she'd have had a fit.

"Keep your skirt down, Sophie!" she would have admonished. "And behave like a *lady!*" Like I said, whatever other faults Sophie's mama had, she certainly raised Sophie to be a real lady.

I don't know why that particular image of Sophie stands out like it does in my mind. But then, we never do know how it's going to be with us when we get older.

Anyway, when she was just a little girl, Sophie used to come over to my house some afternoons, whenever her mama would let her, and she'd play dress-up, draping herself all over with my scarves, and sometimes, I'd let her put some of my face powder on her nose. Other times, she liked just lying across the front of my bed and watching me mending my silk stockings or making some tatted lace for the pillowcases in my hope chest.

"What's a hope chest?" she asked me once. It was a rainy Saturday afternoon, I remember.

"It's where you keep all the things you fix up for when you're a married lady," I told her.

"Is that what you're supposed to hope for? Is that why it's called a hope chest?"

"I think so. And yes, it's what every young lady hopes for."

"Not me," Sophie said in a voice strong with that particular kind of certainty children have.

"Yes—you, too," I assured her, enjoying the little proclamation she had made. And her absolute confidence in it.

"No," she insisted. " 'Cause Mama wouldn't let me."

"She would if you were a grown-up young lady," I explained, and then I amended that: "She *will* when you're a grown-up young lady."

"I don't think so," Sophie said matter-of-factly.

I was really quite amused at her earnestness about it. As I said, she was such a precious little girl. Other folks may have thought that she was plain-looking, but I always thought it was just that she'd never had a chance to be free. Or happy, maybe.

By the time Sophie was a young lady, I was already married and had a home of my own——this house, built by my late husband's grandfather, the one who started this whole town. And I think that one of the reasons Sophie particularly liked calling on me was because she enjoyed being with someone who really had a life of her own, if you know what I mean. Not just living right in the same house where she was born, like she did. Years later, after my husband passed on and when all Sophie's old ladies were gone at last, she just kept on coming to call on me anyway.

Such a *lady*, she was. That's why I don't . . . . Well, I'm not sure what happened. About two years after Mr. Oto first came to work for me, it was, if I'm remembering it right. Because after all, it was such a long time ago.

Right around Halloween, and nobody knew what was coming to us in that terrible December.

Chapter Two

At the front walkway of Miss Anne's house, Mr. Oto, her "Chinese" gardener—as everyone called him, if they mentioned him at all—weeded the border plants quietly and methodically near the street, glancing up from time to time, as he watched for Sophie to pass by on the sidewalk. His glance at her from beneath the brim of his straw hat would be so judicious and so brief, no one could have told that he noticed her at all.

And besides, even though no one knew exactly how old he was, he seemed to display all the mannerisms of an older man: His movements were almost always leisurely and slow, his speech—when he spoke at all—measured and soft, as if the sound of his own voice might startle him. So certainly, he was not a man anyone would expect to notice a lady. But notice her, he always did. And that brief glimpse was all he ever expected to have, for after all, she was a real lady—almost old enough then to be called one of the town's matrons. And he was only a gardener. And poor. And finally, not even of her race.

The one and only time he had called himself to her attention in any way was the first time he ever saw her, only a few days after he moved into the cottage behind the back wall of Miss Anne's garden. One of the first jobs she gave him was replacing the broken faucet in the backyard, and so she sent him to the hardware store down the street to buy a new spigot.

As it happened, Sophie was in the hardware store that same day, looking over a display of seed packets near the front door. When Mr. Oto saw her for the first time, she was holding a packet of yellow zinnia seeds in one hand and a packet of sunrise-pink petunia seeds in the other and tilting her head a little as she tried to decide between them. Mr. Oto had never seen such a lovely lady before, and he came very close to staring at her—could not seem to tear his eyes away from the impeccable white lace collar on the dark blue dress and the rich, chestnut-brown hair that was only lightly touched with gray on the deep waves that framed her face. And the deep, mature eyes that were an incredible shade of green—as dark as the leaves of oleander trees. Finally, he cast his eyes down, where they belonged, and as if in a dream, he passed by her and went to find the clerk.

By the time the new spigot was in his hand, Mr. Oto had regained his composure—or so he believed. Because when he turned to leave, he had no intention whatsoever of saying one word to the beautiful lady who was still studying the seed packets. But as he passed so near her on his way out, he watched in horror as his hand came forward with a mind of its own, and his thick, soil-stained finger lightly tapped the packet of pink petunia seeds in her hand.

"Beautiful," he murmured, not knowing if he was speaking of the flowers at all.

Of course, he startled her, even as he startled himself with such an unintentional gesture, so that the first time her eyes turned fully on him, they were filled with offended surprise, and her cheeks instantly flamed into a more vibrant pink than the petunias on the packet. Mr. Oto's own face began to burn at the realization of what he had done, so that just as abruptly as he had intruded upon her privacy, he bowed deeply before her.

"Please excuse me," he whispered, and scurried from the store without glancing her way again.

On his way back to Miss Anne's house, he chastised himself mercilessly. How *dare* he presume to speak to her? After all, he was no impetuous boy—even though he was still young enough for his blood to flow hot in his veins on rare occasions. But he was, after all, mature, and with over fifty years of discipline in him. So there was no excuse for it.

But for days afterward, he found it impossible not to think about her and wonder why she had no husband—as he knew by the absence of a ring on her hand. How could the men of the town, those who were worthy of her—the bankers and the managers and the quiet gentlemen—fail to see the beauty of a face that reflected mature wisdom and gentleness? Why had they never seen it! For she was definitely a spinster, not a widow. He knew that because of the faint aura of expectancy that still clung to her.

In those first few days, he thought about her so often that he even found himself fantasizing about what could be possible if he were not so poor and so old and if only she had come into his life when he had been young and straight. And if only he were wealthy.

"Good morning, my dear Miss Sophie," he would have said, standing tall and strong in front of the gates of his vast estate, wearing a beautiful, embroidery-encrusted coat and bowing low before her. *"I hope this day sees you in excellent health."*

The English would flow softly and easily from his mouth when, in truth (although his English was exceptionally good), it was not the language of his childhood in his father's house, so he had never felt completely comfortable with it. But in his daydream, English was completely easy and natural for him—because it was Sophie's language.

"Good morning, my dear Mr. Oto," Sophie would have answered in a voice softened around the edges in the way of Southerners, and then, to his delight, she would have blushed and fluttered a little—prettily—walking toward him the whole time and with the soft folds of her summer dress flowing around her.

But those images set his heart to thudding ominously and caught and held his breath against the thuds, so that finally, he disciplined himself against feelings that had come far too late in his life and for a lady who would have been completely unattainable anyway. So that never again in those years since he first saw her had he spoken to her or tipped his hat or called her attention to him in any way.

The only thing he allowed was that he weeded Miss Anne's front walkway every weekday morning, when Sophie was likely to pass by, but even then, when she was so near, he tended the plants as if they were the only important things in the world—working his thick fingers into the soil around them and waiting to take the brief glance at Sophie that was all he would ever have. So that particular October morning, as usual, he weeded and waited and wondered what she would be wearing and where she would be going.

Sometimes, she wore a wide-brimmed hat with tiny silk flowers on it and a voile dress—that was usually on Tuesdays, when she went to the book discussion meeting at the library. Other mornings, she wore baggy men's coveralls—even then, somehow managing to convey an impression of complete elegance—and carried a crab trap. That's when she was on her way to tend the traps she set in the creek that ran through the marsh at the edge of town. At those times, he envied even the crabs she would reach in to grasp, take out of the trap, and declaw on the spot.

On Wednesdays, she wore the same dark blue dress she had been wearing that infamous morning in the hardware store—but with a variety of tatted or crocheted collars, all pristine and immaculate. That's when she came calling on Miss Anne, opening the gate and coming right up the walkway, her feet passing—*incredibly!*—within inches of his busy hands, and the delicate wake of her cologne wafting over him where he knelt, weak-kneed, among the marigolds. The first few times she came into the yard like that, he was terrified that she would remember him as the one whose rude behavior had so deeply offended her, but if she remembered, she never gave the least indication of it. In fact, she never looked his way at all.

On this custom of "calling," Mr. Oto had once asked Matilda, who came to Miss Anne's house once a week to clean and do the laundry.

"What do you mean?" Matilda demanded of him, suspiciously, when he asked her about it. She was ironing a damask tablecloth and, as usual, thumping the heavy iron down upon the cloth hard enough to make the ironing board shudder on its wooden legs.

He was hesitant to continue, for Matilda's open contempt frightened him. After all, he had heard her refer to him as that *"ugly, dried-up, yellow foreigner."*

"Please . . ." He pressed forward with it, in spite of Matilda's scowl. "Why do ladies come here sometimes?" He was trying to keep the question very broad, although he knew and Matilda knew also, that no other ladies from the town ever came to call on Miss Anne.

Matilda slammed down the iron against the board once again, only harder than ever, and turned to face him, threatening and ominous.

"Folks just come calling," Matilda spat out the words at him, as if they explained everything. "Don't you know nothing at all about good manners?"

And because he didn't know how to answer her question, he said nothing more.

Other times—when Sophie wasn't coming to call—she wore sandals and a voluminous paint-stained blue duster and carried an easel under her arm and a paint-spattered wooden case from which he could hear the rattle of brushes. That's when he knew that she was going to paint watercolor pictures at the river.

In fact, Mr. Oto sometimes went down to the river himself to paint delicate watercolors of marsh grass and to try to capture the glint of infinitesimal sky in the water and to pretend that Sophie was sitting there beside him. But he always made sure that he would never intrude upon her singular right to that place by the river, because he went to it only on Sunday mornings, when Sophie was usually within the confines of the Salty Creek Baptist Church.

At a few minutes after ten o'clock, he heard Sophie's footsteps on the sidewalk, and then came his careful and brief glance. That morning, she was walking in a preoccupied way, wearing a light blue silk dress and with her arms crossed over a slim book held close to her heart, and her lips were moving soundlessly.

And because he had no idea where she was going at such times, he imagined that she went to a different place near the river, where she sat beneath a moss-laden tree, breathing line after line of poetry into the air. English poetry that he had trouble fully understanding, but that he continued trying to learn—poems that thundered and wept and brought such an exquisite pain to his soul that he could hardly bear it.

So unlike the limited English of his childhood—in a place where English was used only for conducting business and nothing else.

He had asked Miss Anne to bring books of poetry to him from the library, believing deep in his heart that if he could only learn to read poetry such as Sophie read, he would, somehow, be with her. Miss Anne never once suspected that inside the small, intense man was a heart hungry to learn the language of love, and she delighted in bringing him the books he asked for. She sat with him for long hours, watching as his brown finger passed across the page and listening to him sounding out the words. And when he would come to the end of a poem, he would nod his head in deep satisfaction and glance at Miss Anne with shining eyes.

That particular morning, he suddenly remembered some of those beautiful words. And so he whispered, "My heart leaps up when I behold a rainbow in the sky!"

The words of Wordsworth's poem echoed most pleasantly through Mr. Oto's mind as Sophie walked away down the sidewalk, and more—the words seemed to course through his brown arms in warm rivulets and to run out from the tips of his fingers so that he could feel their beauty draining into the earth around the marigolds.

"These flowers will be especially beautiful," he whispered. "I will be able to look at them and see which ones were watered with such words."

Mr. Oto did not know then that the crisp, October day would present yet another miracle to him—besides his glimpse of Sophie and his belief that marigolds could absorb through his own fingers the very beauty of the words.

For her own part, Sophie seldom noticed Miss Anne's gardener in the front yard when she passed by the house or when she came to call. But she certainly remembered him. Particularly she remembered his audacity in trying to tell her which seeds to buy. *For goodness' sake!*

But she also remembered that horrified look in his black eyes when he realized his infraction, and his deep and completely apologetic bow. After he had left the hardware store that day, Sophie decided upon the petunia seeds after all—and *not* because some strange, foreign man had said that she should choose them. And she wondered only briefly how someone like him had come to live in their little town, anyway.

Later, a bit of that story about Mr. Oto came to her, unbidden, at a Garden Club meeting she went to in the company of her Aunt Minnie, who was already too frail and confused, even back then, to be going anywhere. But her aunt had threatened to cry if she couldn't go, so Sophie took her—but thankfully, only that once. Sophie found it to be almost unbearable, sitting still for so long inside the Community Center on such a beautiful day, listening while the speaker droned on and on about composting and drainage, and all the while, through the window, she could see the green fronds of palms against the blue sky and a few moisture-laden clouds gathering in the south.

At the end of the meeting, Miss Anne told Sophie's Aunt Minnie—quite grandly and with her voice loud enough to carry to everyone else—that she had been fortunate enough to find a "real Chinese" gardener.

Across the room, someone whispered, "I've seen him, you know, and I declare, he's the strangest-looking bandy-legged little man!"

"I've seen him, too, and I think he's a colored man. At least he's certainly very dark!"

"And where did he come from? Does anyone know? Anne's awfully foolish to have the likes of *him* living right behind her own garden!"

But Miss Anne ignored what they said, if indeed she heard them at all.

And before long, the full story of how the strange foreigner came to live in the little town of Salty Creek was common knowledge, thanks primarily to Eulalie, the doctor's wife, who, though a good and kind lady, was prone to talking loudly to anyone about anything, especially when she was sitting under the roaring hair dryer in the beauty shop.

Chapter Three

*M*iss Anne said:

Lord knows what kind of stories Eulalie was telling. She always did have a flair for the dramatic, and whenever she started in to telling something—well, if she thought it wasn't quite good enough, she'd fix it up a little bit. You know how it is. But she certainly didn't mean anything by it, and goodness knows, she was the first one to befriend Mr. Oto. Didn't care one little bit about him being a foreigner. Or about him not being white. Which is a lot more than I could say about some of the others around here.

Because this is a small town. A simple town. With whites and blacks who know how to get along together. Back then, it was a different way of getting along, because everybody knew what all the rules were, and they *were* rules, you know, even though they weren't written down anywhere. Not that I ever knew of. Most folks never questioned them, either. Because it was just the way things had always been done. So white men ran the town and black men worked in the fish-packing plant; white women stayed at home in their houses—particularly in hot weather—and black women came to those houses every day, to cook and clean.

Then along came Mr. Oto, and he sure upset the applecart! Because he wasn't what any of us knew, and he didn't seem to fit in with any of those rules at all. Brown as a biscuit, he was, and small. Probably not more than five feet tall. Stocky, though, and with those slanted-looking eyes. And all that bowing he did all the time!

Why, no one in this little town had ever seen anything like him. And it was probably very much to his advantage that he was always a very quiet and private person. Unobtrusive, you might say.

But the way he came to be here in Salty Creek in the first place was that he was on a Greyhound bus that always passed through Salty Creek—back then, anyway—on the way to Jacksonville. Started in New York City. That far away. But that time, when the bus was only a few miles outside Salty Creek, one of the passengers came up front and told the driver there was a foreign man on the bus who was sick. So when the bus made its usual just-before-dawn stop at the Gulf station here, the driver called the sheriff, which was all he knew to do. Told him that some of the passengers were scared the man had plague or something like that. For after all, he certainly was a foreigner.

The sheriff came right away, wearing a raincoat over his pajamas, and all he could learn from the others was that the man boarded the bus in New York City and hadn't seemed to be sick then. Just real tired, the other passengers said.

But when the sheriff went onto the bus and picked him up, he noticed right away that he was real frail—no bigger or heavier than a child, the sheriff said. So it was easy to carry him off the bus and put him in the backseat of the patrol car.

He also said that something or other about the whole thing felt kind of strange to him, so he waited long enough to watch the bus pull out of the Gulf station and roar away into the darkness—and all those faces staring from behind the windows were glowing just like lanterns. I told the sheriff that sometimes strange things like that happen, especially when something unexpected comes out of the dark.

He took Mr. Oto—although he didn't know his name then, of course—straight to the doctor's house, and after looking him over, the doctor said he couldn't find a thing wrong with him except that he probably hadn't had anything to eat in goodness-knows-how-long. That, and a bruise on his head, maybe from having fallen down sometime.

"He just needs something to eat and some rest," the doctor said. "And we need to keep an eye on that bruise, too."

About that time, Eulalie came to the door of the office, to see what kind of patient was coming before it was even daylight. She always was curious about things, you see. And when she heard what the doctor said, she went right into the kitchen and heated up some leftover gumbo, adding a little water to it so Mr. Oto's empty stomach wouldn't rebel at it, especially if he hadn't had anything to eat in a long time.

She told me later that when she brought the gumbo to Mr. Oto, it almost broke her heart, seeing that strange, dark face against the white pillowcase and him shivering under the sheet, just like it was the dead of winter. Said that when she started feeding him that good gumbo, he opened his mouth for her—just like a baby bird, she said—and she could actually see the broth warming him up, and those black eyes losing the frantic look they'd had before, so that they even seemed to be growing larger, and warm, and soft. But that may have been Eulalie's imagination getting the best of her.

Still, by the next morning, he was much better. But when the doctor started asking who he was and where he was going on that bus, Mr. Oto just smiled and shook his head and said nothing—except to touch his chest and say, "Oto." That's how come the doctor figured he didn't speak any English. So he communicated with Mr. Oto from then on by using his hands a lot and short, simple words, too, which he yelled—just as if the man were deaf.

Eulalie certainly went into a flurry of cooking over the next few days, and all in Mr. Oto's behalf. Always like that, Eulalie was—had a big heart for creatures that were sick. Or lost.

Why, one time, she had a whole bunch of seven or eight stray cats she fed all the time. And she had names for every single one of them, too. Used to cook up a concoction of pigs' livers and oatmeal for feeding to them. What a smell that was! And it was only after all the doctor's patients started complaining to him that he had to put his foot down about that.

And I'd expect that the minute the sheriff brought Mr. Oto in, the good doctor knew what was going to happen, as far as Eulalie was concerned.

She sure lived up to her reputation that time, because for breakfast she fixed steaming bowls of grits, platters of fried eggs, and plates piled high with hot, buttered biscuits. For noontime dinner, she made fried chicken or chicken with dumplings or meatloaf and always a big bowl of mashed potatoes that towered above Mr. Oto's smiling face where he sat at her table. For supper, she served cold fried chicken and potato salad, or country ham and cornbread, and Jell-O salads that were thick with fruit cocktail. And always, a platter piled high with cornbread and plenty of butter to go with it. That Eulalie sure loved to cook, and she'd been missing it, what with the doctor always being on some kind of diet and trying to watch his weight. Not that it ever did him much good, though.

So Mr. Oto ate and ate, as if he could never get enough, Eulalie said. And the good doctor ate and ate, too—and gained a full six pounds in only a few days. He was already a big man, you see, and with all that good food, he got even bigger in a hurry.

But anyway, that's how Mr. Oto regained his health, so much so that a few mornings later, he swept out the doctor's office and washed all the windows in the whole house, unasked. Then he trimmed the bushes in the front yard, and he found some tomato plants in a can of water on the back porch—the doctor had meant to plant them the weekend before—and he carefully set them out in the back garden. So that the doctor's office was sparkling clean, the garden well-tended, and Eulalie's kitchen just roiling with the good smells of her cooking.

It was no wonder to me that although Mr. Oto was certainly well enough to travel again, he didn't seem to understand that the doctor was trying to suggest that he do exactly that. In fact, whenever the doctor tried to talk with him about it, Mr. Oto looked at him with a blank look on his face, and, of course, Eulalie snorted and glared at the doctor whenever he tried to bring it up.

Finally, the good doctor came to me with his problem, because we'd been friends for many years, and, too, he knew about the gardener's cottage on my property. And, as he said, Mr. Oto couldn't go on forever sleeping on the cot in the back of his office. Of course, I had been expecting it, really—what with all the fuss Eulalie was making over Mr. Oto—so I agreed to let him stay in my cottage until he was ready to continue his journey. And besides, the doctor knew I wouldn't mind if Mr. Oto was a foreigner. And that he wasn't white.

But because I was never one to receive charity or to

give it, I said he'd have to earn his keep by working for me——replacing that broken faucet in the backyard and the cracked windowpanes in the sunroom and by painting the front porch, too.

Poor Eulalie put up a terrible fuss when the doctor told her Mr. Oto would be leaving their house, and finally, the only thing that would stop all her crying and carrying on was that the doctor and I agreed that she could continue providing Mr. Oto with sumptuous meals. For a while, at least.

All in all, it seemed to be a pretty good solution, and so the doctor delivered Mr. Oto to me. I hadn't seen him before myself, and I'll have to admit that I'd never seen anyone who looked quite like him before. Still, he looked quite nice in the doctor's freshly washed and ironed, outgrown clothes and carrying a bulging, brown-bag lunch. Just to tide him over until Eulalie could deliver his supper.

But the funny thing was this: As soon as the doctor left——and all that leave-taking required a lot of smiling and bowing on Mr. Oto's part——he turned to me, and bowing once again, he said in the softest possible voice . . . and in perfect English, "I am most grateful for your generosity."

At that, I pounced on him with a lot of questions—— after finding out that he could speak English as well as an American. But instantly, he retreated into all that silence and bowing. So in that quiet way, he let me know that he wasn't going to say much about his past. Or his future either, for that matter.

Well, I accepted that about him because I don't like telling people my business, either. So he moved into the small stone cottage behind my garden wall and seemed to be pleased with it. It was almost a year before he asked me for anything other than what I put into the cottage for his use: a cot, a table, two chairs, and—to his obvious delight—wood for the fireplace for when the nights would be cool in winter.

Within the first few days, he fixed the broken faucet and replaced the cracked windowpanes in the sunroom and painted my whole front porch without spilling so much as a drop. When all that was finished, he started in to weeding the big back garden—without being asked. And he did a beautiful job of it. Why, the flowers fairly leaped into bloom under his hands. And goodness knows, no one had cared for that garden in years. Not since my husband passed on. Made me feel so good to see it pretty and clean again, and with the flowers just blooming to beat the band.

From the very beginning, Mr. Oto was such a completely delightful man—quiet and unobtrusive, and above all, exquisitely polite—that I really became quite fond of him. So I bought a straw carpet to cover the bare, plank floor of the cottage and gave him a small electric plate so that he could make tea for himself.

For the longest kind of time, good old Eulalie continued to deliver at least one sumptuous meal to my house every day, and Mr. Oto dined, alone, on my back porch. Later, when the winter came and some of the days were quite chilly and very rainy, I fixed a card table for him on the sunporch, so that he sat among all those neglected plants I meant to find time to work with—and he always took a few minutes before he ate to pluck the dead leaves from them and to loosen the packed and dried soil in their pots. Soon, they were blooming also.

Finally—somehow—both Mr. Oto and I seemed to take it for granted that he would stay. And he did.

Chapter Four

After Sophie's footsteps faded away, Mr. Oto went on with the work he had planned for that day, placing six new pink dogwood saplings almost tenderly in the wheelbarrow and pushing it along the driveway, gazing somewhat sadly at the young trees, at their leaves shivering with the bumping of the wheel, almost as if they were shuddering of their own accord. For he knew, as he always knew, that Miss Anne would have him plant them without thought of line or composition or texture or meaning.

Better, he was thinking, *to have one and only one such tree, with silence and space around it, so that in the spring, its blossoms will be like pink stars in an empty sky.*

That's how he would have planted the garden. But he could not say that to Miss Anne, because it would be rude of him to try to tell her. And after all, she had befriended him, so it would seem to be ungrateful as well. And besides, he was only a gardener. So it wasn't his place to say anything like that.

But the trees know. And so do I.

He knew because of his father's small garden behind the house in California, where he had grown up. So that from the time when he was very young, his father had taught him how to work with the soil and the plants and to create something that would be beautiful to gaze upon. How could he ever forget the beautiful little pool right in the garden's center, and the few, beautiful goldfish in it? Then he imagined Sophie's face—solitary in his mind against a background of sheer emptiness—his having finally found someone whose face was worthy of that shrine within his being. Someone incredibly beautiful—but found too late in his life. And a woman unattainable to him anyway.

That's what was on his mind when he pushed the wheelbarrow into Miss Anne's back garden, and he was so intent upon his vision of Sophie's face that when he looked up and saw a great crane of Japan standing there, it took more than a few moments for him to realize exactly what was right there before his very eyes, standing just as still as a statue at the very back of the garden, its feathers as motionless as if they had been painted onto the backdrop of the black-green camellia leaves.

Mr. Oto staggered to a stop and gazed at it, while the full realization of what he was really seeing came very slowly, along with the memory of his father's voice, speaking very long ago, saying: *"When I was just a child, my father took me once to the island of Hokkaido. And there, I saw the great cranes of Japan dancing in the snow."*

He blinked several times, as if to clear his vision, and then he began arguing against the very existence of that distinct, clear, and majestic creature.

It could be a blue heron, perhaps—a larger one than I have ever seen before. Or maybe an egret with very strange plumage. But not a great crane of Japan. Impossible!

Indeed, herons and egrets sometimes came into the gardens and yards of the houses in that small town so close to the salt marshes—great blue herons and snowy egrets came, but never a great crane, such as Mr. Oto had never seen, but that his father had described to him in great detail.

But the crane still stood in his direct view—absolutely real, to the denial of all other possibilities. So that finally, he knew that he was not dreaming. It was real. A great crane of his father's homeland. The slender neck and the unmistakable red spot on the white head and the gash of black feathers against the neck and along the tail.

And the sheer size of it! At least five feet tall, Mr. Oto guessed. Exactly as tall as Mr. Oto himself.

"Mr. Oto? Mr. Oto?" Miss Anne's voice called his name not once, but twice—as always. So that no matter how close he was, he never had time to answer her until she had called him a second time.

Behind him, the screen door slammed and Miss Anne's gardening boots clumped noisily on the wooden steps. She was coming to give him minutely detailed instructions about where she wanted him to plant the dogwoods, and how deep she wanted him to dig the holes, and how often he must water them.

And the crane, hearing the noise, looked once more directly at Mr. Oto for a long moment before it moved slowly in and among the camellia bushes until he could see it no longer.

"Mr. Oto? Mr. Oto?" Miss Anne called again from the bottom of the steps.

"I am here, Miss Anne," he finally said in a voice too low for her to hear. "I am here. But I am not here."

I am with my father when he was a child in faraway Japan, a place where I have never been; and with my father's father, whom I have never met; and watching the great cranes—which I have never seen—dancing in the snow.

"What on earth are you doing, Mr. Oto?" Miss Anne came to stand directly in front of him and to lean forward, studying his face in nearsighted concern. "Are you ill? You look as if you've seen a ghost!"

"No, miss," he finally managed to say, but still, he did not look at her, but leaned a little to see the camellia bushes and to wonder if there was something hiding in them.

Or am I becoming a dream-laden man who can't tell what's real? Like my old father before me?

Miss Anne looked at the bank of camellia bushes against the wall. Nothing was there.

"Well, then, if you're sure you're all right, let's get these dogwoods planted before the roots dry out any more," she said, striding off toward the other side of the yard and then looking back at him expectantly. Like an obedient child, he followed her. But to himself he said, *What can it mean that a great crane has come to me here? And what message does he bring—of my father and of my father's ancestors?*

Chapter Five

*M*iss Anne said:

Only once in the two years Mr. Oto lived in the gardener's cottage did he ever ask for anything other than what I provided for him. But one Sunday evening at dusk—about a year after he came—he called to me from the back steps and stood with his hat in his hands and asked me if he could build a small hut behind the cottage.

"A hut?" I wondered if I had heard him right. "Why on earth would you want a hut, for goodness sake? You have a nice cottage to live in."

That's what I asked him.

As usual, Mr. Oto was gazing down at his shoes. It was always hard to get him to look me right in the eyes.

"Not a hut for living in, please," he said. "A hut for thinking."

That sure didn't make any sense to me at all, so I tried a different tack: "What *kind* of hut?" I asked, and to be truthful, I was feeling a little bit alarmed, because I was thinking that maybe he would nail together a bunch of old boards or something like that. An eyesore to the neighborhood, even though the land behind the gardener's cottage wasn't easily visible from the street. Still, I had a responsibility to the town, you see.

"A hut of wooden poles and a roof of palm fronds that have already fallen from the trees. A very simple hut, please," Mr. Oto persisted.

"A hut?" I asked once again, because it was really confusing to me, you see.

Mr. Oto just nodded, very patiently, it seemed.

"Well, if you must," I finally conceded. "But what do you want it for?"

"For thinking," he repeated.

"You're not going to worship some kind of idol in there, are you?" I asked right out, because I didn't know much about people from China, you see. But one thing I did know was that Mr. Oto didn't go to church on Sundays and didn't seem to be interested in ever going. Because he never once asked me about the time of services or anything like that. Still, I couldn't say a thing about it, because I didn't go to church either. Never have, not since I was a young woman. Seems to me that I can look out my own window and see the flowers and the trees and feel real happy that I'm on this earth, and God and I both seem to like that kind of churchgoing just fine. And it's honest. I'll say that much for it.

So I'd never thought much about Mr. Oto's beliefs except once before—right after he came to live in my cottage. Ruth stopped by one day and said she needed to talk to me about him.

Because Ruth kind of made every single thing that went on in town to be her business. Maybe like a town spokeswoman or something like that. Self-appointed. So it really didn't surprise me that she showed up at my door soon after Mr. Oto moved into the cottage.

Said she wanted to suggest, right off the bat—that's the way she put it—that I get Matilda to take my foreign man over to the African-Methodist-Episcopal church with her. Because that's where he belonged. It was a little church out on the edge of town. A colored church.

Ruth wanted to suggest that right away, she said, before I could tell him it was all right for him to go to the white church. I guess Ruth was just assuming that, eventually, he would want to go to church somewhere, just like everybody else in this town. Except me. And Eulalie, too, come to think of it.

"And what's wrong with him going to your church?" I asked her that day. Of course, I knew what she thought was wrong with that, and truthfully, I came right out and asked her because I wanted to see her squirm. And sure enough, she started squirming right away, and I'm sorry to say that I enjoyed every minute of it.

"Why, Anne!" she fairly sputtered. "He certainly can't come to *our* church!"

"But why not?" I asked in an innocent voice, and I particularly enjoyed driving *that* nail home.

"You know perfectly well why not!" She lowered her

voice, as if she were revealing a deep, dark secret. "He's not *white*!"

"And he's not *black*, either," I whispered back, as if that, too, were a secret. Then I paused for a moment before I added, "And I strongly suspect he's not even a Christian, at all, so you can stop worrying about him wanting to come to *your* church."

Well, that certainly set her back, I should say, and I could see a terrible struggle going on inside her—between her "Christian duty" to bring this errant lamb to the fold of Christ's flock and her blatant determination that he not enter that fold on a path that led through the *white* church.

But I couldn't bear watching her dilemma any longer, because somehow, all the pleasure had gone out of it. "Just leave him alone, Ruth. I don't think he wants to go to any church at all."

About that time, Mr. Oto knocked on the back door, and Ruth followed me as far as the kitchen and waited there while I went to the door. And the whole time Mr. Oto and I were discussing what to do about a diseased oleander, she watched him as if—given the right opportunity—he would drink blood and howl at the full moon.

Why, if he had said *Boo!* she would have run right into the doorjamb! I guess by that time, though, she'd made up her mind to forget about trying to save his soul—because she never brought up the subject of Mr. Oto's going to any church again. In fact, I don't think she ever looked at him after that day. Maybe she decided to pretend that he didn't exist. *That* certainly relieved her of her "Christian duty"!

But anyway, that's why I had to make sure that if I gave him my permission to build this hut of his, he wouldn't be worshiping an idol in it or anything like that. For it might have attracted Ruth's attention and maybe even brought her descending upon me once again. I certainly didn't want that to happen.

"Not worship an idol," he assured me, and he only thought he was hiding that smile of his from me.

Well, I was thinking, *if he isn't going to worship an idol and the hut can't be seen from the street anyway, what harm can it do?*

"All right," I said at last, and I sighed loudly enough to discourage him from asking me for anything else and went back into the house, leaving him bent in a deep bow and still smiling at the ground. Always did drive me crazy, that did. All that smiling he did all the time. And the bowing.

And like I said, people around here never did get used to him—or even try to get to know him at all. I guess either they thought he was a heathen, like Ruth did, or else they couldn't get past the color of his skin—a very deep honey-brown. Not quite dark enough to be thought of as black. But certainly not light enough to be called white, either. And the dark, slanted eyes that—really—were quite kind, if you took the time to look at them and to get close enough to him to do that.

I took quite a bit of criticism, sure enough, letting him stay in the gardener's cottage behind my back wall.

But for the most part, folks around here were used to my doing things they thought were controversial. Because I never thought anyone—especially me—should live a whole lifetime doing things the way other folks thought they should. I tried to teach that to Sophie, too, whenever I had the chance. But I don't know that she ever really learned it. Like I say, her mama kept her real close. And she raised Sophie to be a lady, too—so in that case, it certainly *did* matter what other people thought.

Chapter Six

About the same time that Mr. Oto first saw the great crane in Miss Anne's garden, Sophie passed the last bungalow at the end of the street and walked beyond, following a curving, unpaved road that meandered off through the palmettos and Australian pines. Still walking somewhat dreamily—as Mr. Oto would have described it—she finally came to a grove of live oak trees near the salt marsh, where she kept a canvas sling chair for just such mornings as that—a morning made for reading and thinking and listening to the scurrying of nameless creatures in the undergrowth. And for gazing across the saw grass to the great, open dome of sky that she always believed was directly above where the river emptied into the ocean.

Here, she could always find a certain quietness of soul, something to restore her so that she could tend the crab traps and plant the new azaleas and figure out how she could stand to read *A Farewell to Arms*. Especially that part in the story where the lovers are parted by such a tragic death.

Sophie avoided tragic love stories of any kind, and in particular, one such as this—that was also about war. And after all, wasn't war the very subject everyone was trying to avoid? What with everything going on in Europe? She had tried to object—politely, of course—when Miss Ruth suggested that novel as the next work to read and be discussed by the book discussion group, but Miss Ruth had insisted they read it. It wasn't lost on Sophie how her eyes glittered when she argued for the book. Titillation, of course—that's what the old lady was after. Titillation over death. And war. And tragic love.

Sophie had never liked Miss Ruth, but of course, she had always been polite to her. Sophie's mama had insisted on that.

"You be polite to her, Sophie. She's your elder and, I might add, a very well-respected lady in this town. I won't have her saying that I haven't raised you right."

"Yes, ma'am," Sophie always answered, but privately, she thought that maybe Miss Ruth wasn't as well respected as her mama thought—that maybe everyone really felt about her as Sophie did, that she was an insufferable busybody who snooped around all the time, trying to cause trouble.

Even when Sophie was a child, she felt that way about Miss Ruth—and with good reason. How well she could remember one particular day when she was only six or seven years old, and Miss Ruth came to see her mama, and they spoke in low whispers in the parlor before her mama called her into the room.

"Sophie, have you been playing with those colored children down by the bridge again? And after I told you not to go down there?"

Sophie had felt her face beginning to burn, and she glanced at Miss Ruth, who was sitting very straight and rigid—just like a skinny, old-lady judge or something—and with her eyes glittering in delight to see Sophie pinned and squirming under her scrutiny and that of her mother.

"Yessm," Sophie muttered, somehow seeing the dark, smiling faces of the children she loved playing with, children of a woman who ran a small crab-house restaurant all alone in her little house near the bridge over Alligator Creek. The long, lovely afternoons of swinging in an old tire that hung from the limb of an oleander tree, and the laughing and the running, the tantalizing aromas of deep-fried fish and hush puppies that came from the kitchen of the little house.

And especially, Sally—her best friend. Sally with the serious face and wearing the red rag wrapped around and around her head that her mama made her wear. Her friend Sally. Queen of the backyard, wearing a bright red, cotton crown.

Queen Sally, Sophie used to call her. Queen Sally with her bright red crown.

"Sophie, are you listening to me?"

"Yessm."

"Don't go there again. It isn't proper."

"Yessm."

"I don't want to hear of you playing with those dirty children again."

"Yessm." *They're not dirty, Mama. They're my friends.*

Miss Ruth—the ruthless witness—nodded her head once, emphatically, and then Sophie's humiliation ended when her mama nodded, too.

"Go on, then. But you mind me now."

"Yessm."

Released to the relative freedom of her own backyard, Sophie sat in her painted-plank swing for a long time, but not swinging. No one to take turns with her. No dark, laughing children. No Sally with her young mouth always in a straight and serious line.

But Sophie refused to cry. Because crying would mean that Miss Ruth had won. And once again, Sophie wondered what kind of power it was Miss Ruth had over everyone. Including her mama.

Who cares what she thinks, that old bag!

But certainly, Sophie's mama cared. And so all because of Miss Ruth, Sophie lost her only playmates and her very best friend. Later, someone said that Sally's mama had closed the crab house and moved with all the children to her sister's house in Augusta. But Sally's solemn face had floated in Sophie's memory for many sad months before, finally, it dimmed and then faded away completely.

And that's exactly what Sophie was thinking about now, all those years later, gazing at those same mean, little, glittering eyes that were now framed in deep wrinkles and gold-rimmed spectacles. But what Sophie didn't know was that the glitter in Miss Ruth's eyes was for titillation all right, but it was titillation for Sophie's suggestion that they read something else. That, and the nearly imperceptible quaver in Sophie's voice.

After the meeting that day, Miss Ruth and her old-lady friends—as Sophie thought of them privately—walked back down the street together and engaged in a far more interesting discussion than any book could have provided.

"I tell you, there's something in her past," Miss Ruth whispered. "It was a tragic love affair. I just *know* it."

"Sophie? A love affair?" another said, incredulously, as if it were something she couldn't imagine in her wildest dreams. "You know good and well her mama wouldn't have put up with anything like that! And besides, when would Sophie have had time for an affair, what with her taking care of all those old ladies?"

"Well, she could have," Miss Ruth argued illogically. "She was right pretty when she was young. Plain and not much in the way of a personality, but right pretty in a simple way. But of course, that didn't last. Always something of a rebellious child, she was, though her mama sure tried hard to make her into a lady. Those are the ones, you know, always kick over the traces and have real, honest-to-goodness love affairs. She's still like that—why, whoever heard of someone from a good family like her tending crab traps like she does, for goodness' sake? And wearing those awful coveralls, right out in public? Heavens above!"

"Seems there was some talk about her and a young man—just before the Great War."

"I heard it, too, but I never knew who he was."

"One thing for sure . . ."

"What's that?"

"He was one of the boys who didn't come back. Else I expect she would have married him, wouldn't she?"

A silence then, because Miss Ruth certainly didn't have an answer for that, but she was still thinking, *There was something. I'm sure of it!*

In her canvas chair beneath the live oak, Sophie gazed across the saw grass—imagining the ocean that was only a mile or so away, salty-sweet and glittering in the October sunshine. Then wondering idly where the water washing onto the shore had come from—maybe all the way from the shores of the Mediterranean or the smooth, white beaches of Hawaii. Or even the coast of France. Came all that way to merge with the fresh water drifting out of the mouth of the river.

But she couldn't hold that mystic, drifting feeling such thoughts usually produced, and so she watched in disappointment while the feeling dissipated like a cloud that comes up on summer afternoons, one that looks like it is holding rain to pour down upon the waiting earth, but that somehow fails to hold its shape so that it rag-tags along and finally shreds into indistinct white ribbons that float away in the high breeze.

It must be all the news about the war, she finally thought. *And not the idea of having to read about those poor lovers parting. But after all, how can those two things be separated? The radio blares out the news of what's happening in Europe— poor England!—and now the Japanese invading Indochina. Where is it to end this time? Like before, with all those young men crossing the ocean to crawl around in muddy trenches and breathe the poison that wilts their lungs?*

And how very well she could remember the haggard eyes and the wheezing breath of those few who came staggering back from France. And the haunting memory of those who never came home again.

Like Henry.

"Nothing lasts." That's what her mama always said.

But Sophie felt the vague stirring—the one that insisted that he *would* come home. And the pure memory of him descended upon her, even after all those long years, so that she could breathe in his aroma and feel the warmth of his nearness. The rough texture of the wool uniform jacket, hear his vibrant voice, and feel the warmth of his hand holding hers.

But if that miracle were to happen, if he finally came back to her, would he still love her? Now that she had those small lines around her mouth and beside her eyes? And a couple of gray hairs near her temples?

For when she remembered him, she also remembered herself as she had been. Slender, pale arms and dark eyebrows that tilted upward. The firm chin and the deep chestnut shine of her hair.

And why is it all coming back to my mind now? Now that the face looking back at me in the mirror is a stranger's face. The face of someone growing older. All soft in the jowls. And sad.

The forgotten volume of poetry was warm and firm against her breast, and her mind began to turn in slow, lazy spirals ever downward, just like a patient buzzard circling in summer air. So that when she drifted into a light sleep, she was young once again, and pretty. And very much in love.

But, Mama, it isn't like that! He's a very nice boy.

Chapter Seven

$\mathcal{T}$he same day in which Mr. Oto had seen such a miracle as a great crane that had come all the way from his father's homeland—perhaps to tell him something very important—he retired to the hut for thinking, just as soon as he finished planting the pink dogwood trees all in a row, as Miss Anne had directed.

For now, there was something far more important for him to think about than the fact that his vision of a lone, pink tree in a beautiful space would never materialize.

And so he sat very still and with his eyes closed.

This is a profound thing, he was thinking. *To see that which I have never seen, that which I know to be impossible.*

Because Mr. Oto never doubted for a moment that some great significance must be attached to it. Could it be that the crane had come to tell him that he should return to his father's home? But by now, perhaps his father had died. For after all, his father was over eighty years old when he sent his son to New York. And Mr.

Oto also had to face squarely the distinct possibility that if his father were dead, his death could have been a blessing. That he would, at last, have escaped the dishonor his own son had brought upon him.

For the crane brought to Mr. Oto the full clarity of his great betrayal and the terrible pain it brought about, both for his father and for his father's sister . . . an aunt he had never even seen—an elderly woman who waited for him to come to her in New York, sent by her brother to bring the money that would deliver her safely into the hands of the loving family in California.

"Speak to no strangers, my son," his old father had said to him when he sent him to New York to bring home the aunt, and Mr. Oto had protested, but respectfully, of course, "Father, I am a man of over fifty years. I know how to behave."

But the father had persisted. "I hear that the city is full of thieves and murderers. Go quietly, find my sister, and bring her home safely with you. With this deed I charge you."

Mr. Oto remembered those words throughout the long, long journey by bus across the country, sometimes thinking of their wisdom and then again rankling bitterly because they seemed to be words such as a father would speak to a young, impetuous, and completely foolish son—not to him! Not with the maturity of his years!

So that when he arrived in New York, he put away everything his father said, and that was exactly the mistake that cost him everything—his honor, his father's trust, and even perhaps his aunt's one opportunity to join her family in faraway California.

For he had just stepped off the bus in New York when a very well-dressed man came right up to him and offered him the opportunity to gain much more money than he had. Mr. Oto hesitated, but then he thought that perhaps this was a custom of the city—a courtesy extended to strangers from far away. Mr. Oto imagined himself returning to California in triumph—bringing not only his father's sister, but also more money than his father had given to him when he left. How proud his father would be!

So he went willingly with the man into an alley near the station, where two other men were laughing together and having great fun with a wonderful game Mr. Oto never heard of. They were throwing white cubes with black dots on them onto the pavement and then exchanging money, still laughing.

What good luck! he thought—that they were willing to include him in their game, and for only a few pennies. And on the next throw of the cubes, they told him that he had won over ten dollars. When they counted out the pile of dollar bills into his hands, his good will toward those fine fellows nearly brought tears to his eyes. Why at this rate, he would return to his father bearing a great fortune that would assure him of high standing in the community.

On the next roll of the cubes, he won again, and his new friends piled even more bills into his hands. So he reached deep into his pocket and brought out the roll of money his father had given him for purchasing the two tickets back to California—one for himself and one for his aunt.

So suddenly, they were upon him, punching him with their hard fists and cursing and kicking him and . . . worst of all . . . wrenching the money away from his hand. Finally the punching and the kicking and the screaming curses stopped, and he heard them running away. He opened his bruised eyes to see the two white cubes with the black dots on them lying disinterestedly on the ground before him.

When he was able to walk, he wandered around the alley, unsure of what to do. Go to his aunt, who was waiting for him, and confess to her? But then what? The money for their bus tickets was gone. What could he do but reveal his stupidity and his shame right to her face?

No!

All day, he wept and argued with himself, and that night, he slept—still bruised and aching—beneath a cardboard box in another alley. The next day, he moved about the backstreets as if in a daze, trying to think about what he should do, and hating himself for not listening to his father. By afternoon, hunger began to gnaw ferociously at his belly, and he had trouble remembering where he was and what had happened to him.

He began digging through the trash cans that stood behind a restaurant where the succulent aromas of food almost drove him insane, and after his empty stomach lurched in alarm at the amorphous clumps of spoiled food, he found some scraps of bread that were miraculously clean, and he ate them greedily, thinking that it was the best bread he had ever tasted. After he swallowed the last morsel and licked his fingers clean of any stray crumbs, he wept and remembered his father's house and the plentiful food on his father's table. And the faces of his brothers.

The second night, he slept under the same cardboard box and dreamed of the garden behind his father's small house in faraway California, of the bougainvillea and the pink petunias and the tiny pool with water lilies and a few beautiful, small goldfish in it. But in the middle of that beautiful dream, he awakened to loud voices and scuffling and grunting sounds, and he drew himself quietly into a small, quivering ball. But just as quickly as he felt the terrible fear and huddled against it—like an animal hiding under a fallen log—he realized that, truly, he had nothing to fear. The money was gone, and all that was left was his life. At that very moment, should someone have taken that, he would have considered it to be a just repayment for his foolishness. And perhaps even a blessed relief from his suffering.

But whoever was in the alley that night did not look under the box.

At the first gray daylight that came into the alley, Mr. Oto came out from under the box, hungrier than ever. His only thoughts were of food—great bowls of steaming rice and crisp garden vegetables and succulent sauces—but then he saw a black wallet on the ground near the trash cans. He glanced around quickly and then grabbed it, praying that it would contain money for food. Clean food. And hot. *Please! Just a bowl of rice! Clean, steaming rice.*

But the wallet was empty—stripped of everything of value. Still, his fingers prodded relentlessly into the tiny pockets—and found a small, obscure rectangle of cardboard tucked deep into a corner of the wallet. *Cardboard? What good is that?* He had trouble reading the words printed on it, but finally he made them out: ONE WAY, JACKSONVILLE, FLORIDA. A bus ticket.

Despite the desperate and disappointed lurch of his belly—which had anticipated food—he nearly laughed aloud. Providence had given him a way to flee the city, the terrible city full of false friendliness and rotting food in open cans and scuffling and grunting in the dark. He put the ticket carefully away into his pocket and kept his hand over it. He had absolutely no idea where this new place—this Jacksonville—was located, but it was where he would go. Good fortune had provided the way, and he would go.

He brushed off his clothes as well as he was able and straightened his collar before he went back into the bus station—to where he had arrived with his father's money and with great responsibility upon him. And with all his false pride. Once there, he waited for a long time, watching the rivers of people coming and going. Seeing people embrace each other, laughing and crying at the same time. Those were the people who still had families. He saw also others like himself, who had no one to greet them and who moved along with their eyes blank and flat.

Finally, he approached the information window and held out the ticket. The clerk glanced at it briefly and at Mr. Oto for a long, breathless moment before she pointed an indifferent finger and mumbled, "Gate Three."

When he found the gate, the bus was already parked there, purring and waiting—only for him, it seemed. Mr. Oto handed the ticket to the driver, but by then, he was so weak with hunger and shame and relief that he could hardly walk. Still, with whatever remote and final bit of strength he had left, he climbed into the bus, sank into an empty seat, and promptly fell asleep. He slept away the miles and the hours, on his way to a solitary life. One without family or friends. In Jacksonville.

But of course, he never arrived there, but ended up in the little town of Salty Creek, Georgia, where the sheriff lifted him up into his big arms just like a baby and the doctor's wife befriended him—and then later, Miss Anne.

Over a year had passed before Mr. Oto sent a letter to his father, confessing his shameful foolishness, begging his father's forgiveness, and enclosing the money it would take to bring his aunt to California—money he had saved from the very small amount of what Miss Anne called "pocket money," that she gave to him, over and above his use of the cottage. And he told his father all about Miss Anne, the kind lady who befriended him, and of his desire to repay that kindness by restoring her garden. After long consideration, Mr. Oto put a return address on the letter: General Delivery, Salty Creek, Georgia.

For weeks after he sent his confession and the money, he thought that perhaps he would receive a letter in return. He even dreamed the words of his father's forgiveness. And so he went to the little post office often, asking if such a letter had come for him.

Finally, it did come. The envelope was addressed in his father's spidery handwriting and the letter inside was very short: "Come home, my son."

But he had not gone home. He didn't quite know why. Because he always meant to go. But one thing had led to another—the fertilizings and the transplantings and the prunings. And his own desire to leave Miss Anne with a lovely garden she would be able to maintain after he had gone. A garden that would be his gift to her.

Now, a great crane of his father's homeland had come to him in Miss Anne's garden. And what could it mean? What did the crane bring to him, besides the terrible memory of his shame and the reminder of his father's great mercy?

All afternoon, he stayed in the hut, meditating and waiting for the answer. Only when it was night did he creep out very quietly and tiptoe around the wall until he entered Miss Anne's garden from the rear gate. He walked across the manicured oval of grass rimmed by the shrubbery. The garden stood empty and expectant. Under his bare feet, the grass was cool and damp, and his shadow in the moonlight stretched across the whole garden, so that he seemed to be a giant.

"Where are you, Great Crane?" he whispered.

But there was nothing in the garden except his shadow.

Every day, Mr. Oto worked in the back garden, watching and waiting, so that he even sacrificed being able to see Sophie, just so he could see the crane again and learn what meaning it had, this impossible thing.

But the crane did not appear. On Wednesday, a small egret came, very early, for a brief look around the garden, and later that same afternoon, an osprey tilted across the sky. But no great crane. Mr. Oto worked and waited and began to wonder if it had really existed at all.

Every afternoon, he sat quietly in the hut, trying to meditate, but instead, he was thinking and wondering about the crane, so that instead of feeling peaceful, he felt worn and more than a little confused.

On Sunday, in the deepest darkness before dawn, the crane came to him once again, this time in what he knew was certainly only a dream. It entered the cottage and stood gazing down at him where he slept, watching him with great, bright eyes. So that he awakened with a start. Nothing there, of course, except for the silver light of the descending moon lying across the floor.

But the dream left him so filled with longing that he got up and made a cup of tea and took it out into the garden at first light to stand quietly, gazing around at the trees hung with Spanish moss and breathing in the aroma of the nearby salt marsh in the morning air.

Suddenly, he knew where to look for the crane. *Of course! I will go to the river this morning,* he thought. *Perhaps the crane is waiting for me there. After all, a crane doesn't belong in a garden, and if one has come all this way, it would want to be in the marsh by the river.*

He went back inside to get dressed, and at the last moment, he began gathering his paints and brushes. While he waited there for the crane, he would paint a picture of it standing against the familiar backdrop of the live oak trees and the saw grass and the pale blue sky. That, he felt, might even encourage the crane to make itself visible to him again.

As he washed out his cup and thought very hard about painting a picture of the crane, Sophie passed by on the sidewalk, hurrying a little so she could go on through town before people started moving about. After all, it was Sunday—the day for church. And they wouldn't understand, even as she herself didn't quite understand, that on this one morning, at least, she couldn't bear being shut up in the narrow, little white building.

Chapter Eight

When Mr. Oto arrived at the river, he saw Sophie sitting in her canvas chair and dabbing paint onto paper. He was completely surprised to find her there, and he intended to turn around and leave before she saw him. But his feet refused to move, so that he stood immobilized and helpless, looking at where the morning light rested like a veil on Sophie's white arms.

From behind him, he could hear the people in the church singing, "What a fellow-ship, what a joy divine . . ."

And although he never made a single sound, Sophie—unbelievably!—turned and looked squarely at him, as if she had known he was standing there the whole time. No offended surprise in her face this time. Only curiosity.

"Good morning?" She phrased it as a question, so that the words also held the meaning of "What are you doing here?"

"Please excuse me," Mr. Oto mumbled, unable to comprehend that he was actually face-to-face, once again, with his *dear Miss Sophie*, and yet completely determined that he would never repeat his bad manners of their one and only previous meeting.

"I will leave." He heard the words come from his own mouth, but until he heard them, he didn't know what they would be.

"Excuse me?" Sophie called to him, for she wasn't sure she heard what he said. It was the sudden male voice that confused her, though it was so soft, she could barely hear it.

"No . . . *you* please excuse *me*," he babbled, not even understanding, himself, what it was he was trying to say. "I will go."

But once again the voice held her. Something about it was like listening to music and waiting for the deep tones of a trombone to balance the high, lonely violin.

"No—don't go," she said at last. "I see that you have paints and brushes. You'll never find another place for painting like this one. It's really quite the best there is. And I don't mind," she added, surprising herself.

Because why on earth was she inviting him, of all people, to share her precious riverbank? Yet at the same time, she remembered his deep and humble bow in the hardware store. Besides, he would not talk much, and when he did speak, the tone would be nice to hear. And perhaps there would be something comforting in having him nearby.

"I hope this day sees you in excellent health." The

measured words, the gentle tone, the soft sincerity—
she smiled and glanced at him where he bowed low
before her.

"Yes, thank you." Then, without another word, she
turned back to her painting.

For long minutes, she heard no other sound and
thought that perhaps he had left after all. Or perhaps he
was still in the deep bow, waiting for . . . what? Her permission to stand erect again?

Then she heard his pencils and brushes rattling as he
sat down at a respectful distance and a bit behind her and
began to sketch. His heart was pounding so hard that the
collar of his shirt trembled, but still he managed at last
to begin sketching the head and the long, graceful neck
of the crane before his pencil trailed off the edge of the
paper and he found himself watching Sophie far more
than he was looking at the sketch.

And in that very strange way in which it can happen,
he gazed at her for so long that her form began to lose all
logical and rational meaning to him, and so it didn't
really come as a complete surprise to him when he
began envisioning white wings behind her, wings that
echoed the angle of her white arms.

He looked back at his sketch, at the long, graceful
neck of the crane snaking across an edge of the paper, and
he began adding the wings, and below them—and yet a
part of them—Sophie's white arms. So that over the next
quiet hour, the crane in his painting became—somehow—one with her: Sophie sitting in her canvas chair by
the river, with sunlight on her arms, while behind her and

yet with her, dreamlike and indistinct, the great crane stood with its wings outspread and its eyes full of love.

And more. Something that had always been and that he had always known.

Of course! The old fable of the Crane-Wife!

Out of his childhood memory rushed back the old story of the poor woodcutter who rescued a great crane and nursed it back to health. So that by magic, the crane became a beautiful bride for him, bringing him good fortune. And love. The story his father's mother had told to his father and his father had then told to him when he was just a little boy. And that he could now see on the paper.

Well! He didn't try to stop the smile of incredulity that curled about him. *A poor gardener could hope to gain such a woman as this. If a poor woodcutter, why not a poor gardener?*

Then he chastised himself, but gently: *Why, this is the kind of dreaming a young and impetuous man would do, and not a man of mature years!*

He glanced a little nervously at Sophie. *My dear Sophie! What would you think if you knew I were imagining you as my Crane-Wife?*

But Sophie, who seemed to be too deeply engrossed in her painting to notice anything about Mr. Oto, was thinking that actually it was quite nice, having someone there with her—a quiet man. The way it would have been with Henry. It wasn't an entirely unpleasant thing to think about, even though the man sitting near her wasn't Henry—would never be.

She darted a glance at the completely unsuspecting

little man and hid her embarrassed smile. *If you only knew what I was thinking,* she thought with amusement, *it would frighten you right out of your wits!*

For an hour or more, they both painted, saying nothing but ever mindful of each other's presence. Then Sophie began gathering up her paints, and Mr. Oto courteously pretended not to notice. But as she left, she smiled politely at him.

"I have to go now. I hope you enjoy your painting."

"Thank you," he managed to mumble, turning his paper just a bit so that she could not see the sketch of herself as the Crane-Wife from the old tale.

On Monday morning, Mr. Oto worked again in Miss Anne's front yard close to the sidewalk, and when Sophie passed by on her way to tend the crab traps, Mr. Oto's glance at her lingered for a moment, and she caught the flicker of his eyes.

"Good morning," she said, but she neither slowed her steps nor looked directly at him—not that he could tell, anyway. And he did not rise from where he was kneeling in the flower beds. But still, he lifted off his hat and held it over his heart.

"Good morning," he answered in a strong voice to her back and received a nod of her head.

My dear Miss Sophie, he did not add.

The same thing transpired on Tuesday. And Wednesday. And on Thursday and Friday. Always the same. Her barely audible "Good morning," and upon his stronger greeting, the curt nod of her head.

Saturday seemed interminable, for Mr. Oto could find no peace at all in the day. He could think only of Sunday morning and perhaps being with her once again at the river. And so the day before this would possibly happen dragged on, seemingly without end.

Chapter Nine

$\mathcal{M}$iss Anne said:

Late Saturday afternoon, my sink got stopped up, so I went down to get Mr. Oto to come and fix it for me. I knocked on the door, and when he opened it—why, I can't quite describe the look that was on his face. Like maybe he'd been expecting someone. But who?

"Could you come help me get my sink unstopped?" I asked, still wondering.

"Oh, yes!" Why, he seemed excited to be unstopping my sink! But I couldn't have said why. And that wasn't the only unusual thing about that day, sure enough.

I remember it so well. He looked absolutely happy to have something to do. And while he clanked around under the sink and muttered to himself softly—but not in English—I began wondering if he were lonely.

Strange that I'd never wondered about that before, but I hadn't. And now that I think back on it, I guess what happened in the garden the week before started me to thinking, too. When he acted so strange, I mean, like he'd seen something out of the ordinary.

What if he were becoming ill? Who could I call? Did he have any family? And where were they?

So while he finished up under the sink, I decided to invite him to have a cup of tea with me. Then I could ask some questions—very politely, of course. And find out what I might need to know. I put a clean cloth on the kitchen table and set out two cups. I'd certainly never invited a gardener—much less someone who wasn't white—to sit at my own table with me before, but for the life of me, I couldn't imagine why not.

"All fixed." Mr. Oto backed out of the cabinet under the sink, returned the wrench to the toolbox on the floor, and stood up—just as the kettle began to whistle.

"Would you like to have a cup of tea with me?" I tried to sound casual about it, but I realized right away that I'd put both of us in a pretty uncomfortable situation. Because what would happen if he declined my invitation? That would make things awkward between us, sure enough, so I guessed all those unwritten rules about how you're supposed to act around people who work for you had some advantages after all.

"Excuse me?" He seemed so surprised that he even put his finger on his chest as if to ask, "Me?"

I nodded, but much to my alarm, he bowed deeply and then fairly bolted right out of the kitchen. *What on earth?* I went to the window and watched him scurry across the yard toward the back wall and beyond it to the cottage.

Goodness! Who would have thought that he would run away like that?

But in only a few minutes, he came running back, with his face fresh-scrubbed to a glow and his hair wet and combed, and wearing a clean—albeit unironed—white shirt. Well, Mr. Oto may very well have been my gardener, but I know a gentleman when I see one, and it was sure enough a gentleman who came to have tea with me that day.

He sat down in the chair just as gently as if he thought it would shatter at any minute and waited silently while I poured the tea and passed a cup to him. That was quite something to see—his thick fingers grasping that fragile cup. And I was very careful when I brought up the subject that had prompted me to ask Mr. Oto to tea.

"Well, tell me, Mr. Oto," I began, trying to keep my voice light and friendly. "Do you have family anywhere?"

But I saw a flush creeping up under his brown skin, in spite of my care, and so I hastily added, "It's just that I wonder if . . . you're very lonely."

Somehow, the added words soothed both of us.

"I have family," he said, letting his eyes meet mine, but only briefly. "But very far away."

"In China?"

He looked down at his lap and smiled. "No, Miss Anne. Not that far away. I have family in California. I was born there."

"But you've never gone to visit your people, not in two long years," I stated. "Why?" I knew that I was really beginning to pry into his business, but I needed to know.

He waited before he answered, and when he spoke, his eyes remained on the cup in his hands. "Please," he breathed. "I am very happy here."

And somehow, I could tell by the way he said it that he wasn't willing to say anything more about that.

"Well then, I won't mention it again," I said. "I was just worried about you the other day, and I thought maybe I should have a name or an address of someone to contact if you should become ill."

"I am no longer a young man, Miss Anne," he said. "But I am in good health, and I am very happy here with things just the way they are. What I thought I saw the other day was perhaps just something I remembered from an old story my father once told to me."

"I'd like to hear it," I ventured, and he glanced at me, perhaps to see if I was sincere or merely being polite. Convinced of my sincerity, he began the story, and right away, I could sense the magical quality of it.

"On a faraway island called Hokkaido, there are great cranes that are found nowhere else in all the world," he began, warming to his story right away so that he spoke with more animation than I had ever seen before. "The story is about a lonely woodcutter who rescued a great crane that was hurt. And he nursed it back to health."

Here, he paused and looked at me again, and he had the strangest smile on him, as if it didn't quite know how to fit into his face.

"And the crane turned into a lovely bride for the woodcutter, through magic." His words were almost breathless. And then he added, "It's only an old story."

"It's lovely," I said, quite truthfully.

"Well, I thought I saw a great crane in your garden that day."

"One that turned into a young woman?" I asked cautiously.

"No." Again, he smiled, and his cheeks quivered, as if they were surprised by it. "Just a great crane."

"It was a blue heron perhaps?" I offered. "Or a whooping crane, of course? That sometimes happens."

"Perhaps," he said, once again wearing that very strange but lovely smile. Then he pushed back his chair, stood up, and bowed deeply to me. "And now, I thank you for the delicious tea."

Well, after that, I'll have to admit that I thought of us as friends a little. Because I'd invited him to take tea at my own table. And because he had told me that lovely story from his own childhood.

So the next morning—which was Sunday—I awakened early, thinking most distinctly that I really should give Mr. Oto more say-so about how the garden would be planted. Goodness knows, he never said anything right out, but I could tell he had other ideas about it.

In particular, when I told him how I wanted the new dogwood trees planted, he asked me, "In a *row*?" And I could hear the disappointment in his voice. But I was stubborn, as usual. So maybe I should listen to his ideas, at least. For after all, he was a gentleman of impeccable taste.

While I was lying there, thinking, I heard him walk past my window on the gravel driveway—on his way to the river to paint, as he always did on Sunday mornings.

Yes—a gentleman of impeccable taste!

Chapter Ten

When Mr. Oto arrived at the riverbank, Sophie was already there, painting and with the early sunlight in her hair and a breeze off the river lifting a loose tendril of hair at her temples.

Once, in a book Miss Anne had brought to him from the library, he had seen pictures of many great paintings, and now, watching her, he wished deeply that he knew how to paint such magnificent pictures. For surely, only such a painting could do justice to her.

While he stood there, she hesitated in her painting and then once again turned to look directly at him. Her round, pink face, the deep green eyes, the careless way the white, open-collared blouse lay upon her shoulders— all these things worked together so that his face tingled, as if he had been briefly burned by a flash of sunlight.

And once again, in the church, the singing began: *"Love lifted me! Love lifted me! When nothing else could help, Love lif-ted meee!"*

"Good morning," she said. And there was more in those same words than had been in them on the weekday mornings.

"Good morning," he answered, and moved forward as if the painting he would do were the only thing that mattered. And once again, he worked on the painting of Sophie as the magical Crane-Wife in the old fable.

After a few silent hours, Sophie gathered her paints and said, "I have to leave now. I hope you will come again next Sunday."

Mr. Oto stood and bowed deeply, all the time placing himself between Sophie and his painting of her.

"I will come," he answered simply.

Walking back home that day, Sophie carried his presence with her, somehow. So that she could almost feel him walking along beside her, saying nothing. But still, his clean-earth smell was in her nostrils and the sound of his quiet breathing, in her ears.

How strange! she thought.

The next Sunday, they met again and painted silently for hours, after which Sophie leaned back a little and turned her head ever-so-slightly toward Mr. Oto. It was a gesture—a new gesture—one that both of them would be able to accept as a signal for the end of painting and the beginning of speaking. For Sophie had decided that she no longer had to be the least bit concerned that he would intrude upon her reveries by talking too much, and once that concern was put to rest—strangely enough, it left a quiet space inside her that she was ready to fill with his voice.

On that particular Sunday, however, Mr. Oto was deeply engrossed in creating the iris of the great crane, an eye that must be dark but that should not be so distinct as to belie the dreamy, almost illusionary quality of the crane. Black, he finally decided, was too abrupt. And gray would not convey the depth of the eye of such a symbol of love and happiness. Finally, he touched together with the brush a bit of the red and some of the blue, and the resulting deep purple of the crane's eye was so perfectly the effect he wanted that he almost gasped.

"You must be very pleased with your painting," Sophie offered, and Mr. Oto jumped a little, as if he had forgotten for a moment that she was there. And he could hardly tear his eyes away from the soft, deeply passionate gaze of the crane.

"I am pleased, yes," he finally answered.

"May I see?" Sophie asked innocently.

"Oh, no!" The abject horror in his response surprised her "I mean . . ." He seemed to be as surprised as Sophie at the intensity of his words, and he glanced at her with deep apology in his eyes. Hastily, he blew upon the great, purple-hued eye to dry it thoroughly before he closed the art tablet.

"Please," he began again. "It's not worthy."

"But I'm sure it's very good," Sophie said, somehow touched by his obvious embarrassment.

"Please, no." Mr. Oto repeated those words and then no more. But his dark eyes were fully upon Sophie, unblinking and with something in them—a burning sincerity, or something. So that she pressed the matter no further. But she didn't feel offended—not in the least. She, who valued privacy, also respected the same value in him.

Once again, when she arose to leave, he stood up also and bowed low before her, a gesture that both embarrassed and pleased her.

"I'm sorry about not sharing my painting with you," he said.

"It's perfectly all right," she assured him. "After all, it's your painting, to do with as you please. And I'm sure it's quite lovely."

"Thank you," he said. And he did not add, *Lovely—but only because you are lovely.*

Throughout the golden days of November, they met in that quiet and gentle way every Sunday, and in those few weeks, Sophie and Mr. Oto accepted the new routine their friendship had brought. Sophie passed by Miss Anne's house nearly every day, she and Mr. Oto spoke their quiet greetings, and on Sunday mornings, they painted together by the deep and slow-moving river.

At first, they had spoken very few words to each other. But the silence between them was sweet—filled with the distant cries of gulls and the whisperings of the gentle wind in the live oak tree. And little by little, they began to talk, hesitantly and somewhat timidly at first, merely offering small comments about the angle of the sun and occasionally identifying migrating flocks of birds to each other—which reminded Mr. Oto that he had not yet seen the great crane again, that creature he had sought to find at the river and which, now, he had nearly forgotten. Except for the painting.

But as Sunday followed Sunday, Mr. Oto and Sophie began giving bits of old stories of their youth to each other—exquisite, glimmering images of worlds they lived in before their acquaintance. So that Sophie could see him as a small boy, trying to catch the goldfish in the pond in the center of his father's garden. And Mr. Oto knew Sophie as the little girl who loved to run back and forth under the crisp, white sheets hanging on the clothesline.

On the first Sunday in December, Sophie studied him quite openly and frankly, so much so that he felt the tips of his ears burning.

"Is everything all right?" he asked, anxious that she was not ill or perhaps angry with him about something.

"Oh, yes," she fluttered. "It's just . . ."

"Please go on," he urged, wondering if something he'd said or done had disappointed or alarmed her.

But she smiled and shrugged her shoulders a bit. "Well, it's just that I don't know your name. Your full name," she added. "I know something about what you were like as a little boy—because you've told me—but I don't even know your first name."

The burning tips of Mr. Oto's ears began pulsating, and he felt ribbons of blushing heat running up his neck on either side.

"I am so sorry," he mumbled.

"No, please don't be embarrassed," Sophie urged, and before she knew what happened, she reached over and put her hand on his arm. They both just sat and stared at that, and then she slowly removed her hand.

"My name . . . ," he began, "is Grover. Grover Cleveland Oto."

"Grover Cleveland?"

If she laughed, he knew that he would die. But she didn't, even though she lifted her eyebrows a little quizzically.

"Like *President* Grover Cleveland?"

"Yes. Because of my father's pride that his youngest son . . . me . . . that I was born in this country. That I am an American."

"Oh, that's lovely," she murmured. Then she added, "If you're the youngest son, then you must have older brothers. Were they born in China?"

"No. Not China," he said, realizing that Sophie simply believed what everyone else in town believed about him. Even Miss Anne.

"Not China?"

"Japan." How strange the word sounded to him.

"But everybody thinks—"

"I know," he interrupted her gently.

"Why don't you correct them?" Sophie asked.

"Because I do not want them asking questions about me," he confessed. "I am a very private man."

"Oh! I'm so sorry!" Sophie breathed. "Why, I've been as rude as can be, asking you all kinds of personal questions!"

"No!" He hastened to halt such an abject apology. "You are not like them. For you to ask is perfectly fine."

Suddenly, he realized how relaxed and smooth the English words were rolling off his tongue. Exactly as in his daydream.

"Then may I please ask just one more?" Her voice had a playful lilt he had never heard in it before.

"Of course."

"May I call you by your given name?"

"Given name?" He had never heard of such a thing.

"Your first name."

"Yes. Please." But he almost stopped breathing at the thought of the lovely Miss Sophie actually saying his name aloud.

"Grover." Her voice was soft and melodic, like the faint lapping of ripples at the edge of a beautiful marsh deep inside him.

So that all the next week, he heard her voice over and over again, saying his name. And it was enough.

The next Sunday—December 7—Sophie sighed deeply only halfway through the morning and put down her brush. Mr. Oto looked at her where she sat gazing at the sky.

"I have never been able to paint the sky exactly as I see it," she confessed.

"May I look?"

"Of course," she laughed. "*I'm* not timid!" She didn't add, *As you are*. But he could sense her unspoken teasing. So that he smiled as he leaned just enough to be able to see her painting.

"It is good," he pronounced genuinely, nodding his head. "What you have painted is very good."

"But it's not the way I really see it," she explained. "Because the sky that's over where the river and the ocean come together is very beautiful—very different—in a special way. And I just can't seem to get it right, on the paper."

Mr. Oto wiped his brush and put it away before he responded. "Perhaps," he ventured, "that's why it is so beautiful—because it is beyond capturing."

Sophie looked at him in surprise. "Maybe you're right about that." She laughed. "Maybe that's what it is." And to herself, she thought, *How perceptive! And poetic!*

Mr. Oto laughed with her, but a rusty kind of laugh, as if it were something that he had forgotten how to do—if, indeed, he had ever known.

"Some Sunday, perhaps we may walk over to the place where the river comes into the ocean and look most carefully at the sky," he suggested.

Sophie hesitated. "Then would I be able to paint it?" she asked, very seriously.

"Perhaps not. But it would be a fine thing anyway."

"Yes," she finally agreed. "It would be a fine thing. I'd like to do that."

Then, inexplicably, she looked full into his dark eyes. Mr. Oto, caught by surprise, could only gaze back at her. And neither of them looked away.

Once again, when Sophie walked home from the riverfront, she felt his presence go along with her, and she smiled, both at that and at the absolute beauty of the sunny, clear morning. The breeze off the river, with its satisfying aromas of earth and sky and water. Her footsteps in time with the cries of a white gull high overhead and all the world breathing with her.

What a dear, dear man!

Chapter Eleven

When Mr. Oto walked back to his cottage from the river that day, he moved as lightly as if he traveled only along a silent path deep within. For after all, she was speaking openly with him now. With ease. Looking full into his face. Talking about herself without hesitation. Even saying that they could walk together to where the river and the ocean met. It was more than he could ever have hoped for.

In the cottage, he propped up the nearly completed painting and studied it carefully. It was a good likeness of her, he thought. And the ease with which it had appeared! Almost as if it had leaped onto the paper, of its own choice. The image of Sophie sitting in the chair by the river, sunlight on her arms, and behind her—indistinct and dreamlike—the great crane stood with its wings extended and its soulful eye gazing at him.

"What is it you are saying to me?" he asked the

painting. Asked Sophie. Or the crane. Or both. But only the silence of the quiet cottage answered him.

That afternoon, he sat outside in the sunshine, drinking tea and remembering over and over every single moment of a morning that had left him feeling—somehow, sad. But in a lovely and pensive way.

"Mr. Oto! Mr. Oto!" Miss Anne's voice broke through the tea-golden, sun-washed blue sky of his thoughts. The muffled sound of her running footsteps across the garden on the other side of the wall.

Mr. Oto stood up immediately, because of a tone of distress, a note of urgency—perhaps even of fear—in her voice.

"Miss Anne!" he answered, clattering his cup onto the seat of the chair and running to meet her at the gate in the back wall. She was breathless from her unaccustomed lope across the garden.

"Oh, Mr. Oto," she whispered. "Pearl Harbor—"

"Pearl Harbor?" he repeated senselessly, suddenly imagining himself and Sophie sitting together in the sunshine, while pearls washed up on lapping wavelets from the river and piled against their feet.

"The Japanese," she sputtered. "They've bombed Pearl Harbor."

"Bombed?" He parroted the word, but even on his own tongue it made no sense.

"Bombed our base in Hawaii. It's terrible—a sneak attack! We'll surely have war now!"

Mr. Oto began to gain the full measure of the words. *The Japanese . . . bombed Hawaii? But why?*

"And," Miss Anne was calmer now, but nonetheless serious, and she spoke slowly and with her hand on her chest. "One of the first things I thought about was that people will think you're one of them!" She spat the word in disgust. "One of those nasty Japs! They won't understand that you're Chinese. I'm *afraid,* Mr. Oto!"

I must tell her, he thought—because he knew full well that she thought of him as being Chinese. Everyone in town thought of him that way—*except Sophie! Sophie knew about his ancestry!*

That thought was a new and perhaps even more terrible shock than hearing about the bombing in the first place. Sophie! What would she think? Would she ever speak to him again? Would Sophie think of him now as nothing but a "nasty Jap"?

Miss Anne was still speaking, but he couldn't hear a single word she was saying. He could only study her face and watch her tight, angry mouth moving amidst a roaring in his ears that blotted out everything else.

Sophie! I must find you and tell you that I am not one of those people who would do such a thing!

But how? Would she even speak to him? Would she hate him? Would she turn her face away from him?

Through his agonizing questions, Miss Anne's voice slowly became audible again, but her words were like little feathers that simply floated down toward the horrible ache that filled the pit of his stomach and never quite reached it.

"I'm afraid for you," she repeated. "People will be

infuriated about this! No telling what they will do . . . Oh, I have to get back to the radio. I have to find out what's going on."

But still they stood, separated by the iron gate and with Miss Anne searching Mr. Oto's face in a way he had never seen before. And he, for the first time, looked directly back at her with full, dark eyes that did not blink or turn away from her gaze.

Because under all of the agony, a small flicker of rage had grown, a feeling so foreign to him that he didn't even recognize it.

His mouth opened almost involuntarily: "I . . . am . . . an . . . American." He spoke the words carefully, as if he were afraid they would shatter. "I was born in this country, and I am loyal to it."

The strength of his voice surprised her, the words coming distinct and round, like cannonballs. So that she thought: *Who is this man? This man who has taken tea right at my very own table?*

"I am an American," he said again, only this time his voice was softer and strangely calm, and still those dark, earnest eyes seemed to bore into her very soul.

For long, agonizing moments, they stood in the terrible silence, looking into each other's eyes. Then finally, finally, Miss Anne spoke. "Yes," she said simply. "Yes. You're an American."

Her own words seemed to soothe her, and she took a deep breath. "I was just afraid, God forgive me. I was thinking that someone would come and take it all out on you—maybe a mob even, come and . . . hang . . .

you, thinking that you were one of them! I tell you, people will be infuriated by this horrible and cowardly thing!"

"Thank you, Miss Anne, for worrying about me. But I am safe. I am an American."

"But will you promise me that you'll be careful?" she asked. "Some people may not understand that as well as I do."

"I will be careful," Mr. Oto assured her, bowing.

"And that's exactly what I mean," she said in a voice so soft that he could hardly hear it.

"What?"

"The bowing you do. You shouldn't do that any-more."

"Excuse me?" he almost bowed again, but stopped himself.

"We've all seen those newsreels at the movie over in Brunswick, and that's the way those Japs do all the time. Bow and bow at each other." Her voice began to crack. "Bow even to our ambassadors and then turn around and attack us!"

Mr. Oto had never seen her so angry before.

"Pigs!" she spat out the word and then turned and went silently back across the garden.

He stood at the gate for a long time, until his heart slowed its pounding and he could breathe once again. His one thought was that he should go to Sophie right away. But then . . . suppose this terrible news would cause her to end her friendship with him? That, he simply could not bear. But the mere thought of it taught him, once again, the true meaning of a broken heart.

In the end, he did not go to Sophie, could not bear the possibility that she would now hate him. If that happened, it could wait until the next Sunday, when he would go to the riverbank to paint, as always.

And maybe she would come.

And maybe she wouldn't.

Around that same time, Sophie was sitting in a wicker armchair on her sunporch, reading a little, but more often, simply looking out across the backyard and thinking of the beautiful Sunday morning she'd had in Mr. Oto's company.

From the radio in Sophie's kitchen came soft strains of music. But then some static and an excited voice saying something—almost yelling something that she couldn't quite make out. A strident sound that seemed all out of place on such a beautiful afternoon. She waited for the music to resume, but the voice just kept going on and on.

Finally, she got up and went into the kitchen, and in that first moment when she fully comprehended the news about the attack on Pearl Harbor, she felt her world change forever.

War! This will mean war once again. All the fine young men going off to die in distant battlefields. Like Henry.

But then, right away, another thought leaped into her mind:

Grover!

A sudden, loud knocking on her front door and her feet moving mindlessly into the living room. *Grover?*

But when Sophie opened the door, Miss Ruth was standing on her porch, her mouth in an impatient pout and her shoulders huffy and offended-looking.

"Miss Ruth?"

"Yes," Miss Ruth answered. "Who did you think it would be?" she asked suspiciously.

"Uh . . . come in, please."

The polite words came out, despite the turmoil in her heart, and somehow, her mama's voice showed up in her ears: *"You must always have good manners, Sophie!"*

Miss Ruth entered the living room, glancing around as if seeking something to criticize. Sophie still stood at the door, unable to move her feet.

"Sophie? I've come to ask why you aren't coming to church anymore."

"I . . ." Somehow, Sophie couldn't make her mouth work just right.

"Sophie?"

Silence. Only silence.

"What's wrong with you, Sophie? Are you ill?"

"I . . . can't talk right now." The words sounded weak and tired, but inside, Sophie's heart and mind were a jumble of mindless, flapping wings, darting this way and that, flying into each other and then darting off in another direction.

"Sophie? I'm speaking to you! Are you ill?" Miss Ruth's shrill, relentless voice.

"Pearl Harbor!" Sophie finally managed to say.

"What? What are you talking about? Have you lost your mind?"

A terrible sob erupting from Sophie's chest, and her hating herself for it. "The base at Pearl Harbor. In Hawaii. It's been bombed!"

"What? Bombed, you say? Bombed?" Miss Ruth put a shaking hand over her heart. "But *who*? Who would do such a thing? And how do you know this?"

"Radio," Sophie whispered. "On the radio."

"But *who*?" Miss Ruth insisted. "*Who* bombed the base?" Miss Ruth's beady eyes were filled with both alarm and tears.

"Japan." Sophie breathed out the word.

"Oh! My dear Lord!" Miss Ruth's voice caught in her throat.

"Miss Ruth, I'm sorry. I just can't talk right now. Please ma'am, just you go on home and listen to the radio yourself. Please," Sophie added again.

And Sophie was ever so grateful when Miss Ruth started moving toward the door.

"Japan," Miss Ruth muttered, and then she stopped right in her tracks.

"You better stop spending time with that Chinaman of Anne's, right away, Sophie. He's a stranger—a foreigner—maybe even a *spy!*"

Sophie couldn't speak a word.

"You better *stop!*" Miss Ruth warned again in a terrible whisper. And then she was gone.

On her way back through the kitchen, Sophie turned

the radio off. But the words and their terrible images still remained in the room:

Sneak attack!

Bombs falling!

Ships burning!

Sophie went back to the sunporch, where she had been sitting so peacefully. She stared silently at the chair she had been sitting in, the book she had been reading, the cup of tea on the table—all things from what felt like a different world, with everything now divided into *before* and *after*.

And Grover. What about her dear friend Grover?

"No," she whispered. "Not Grover, but just Grove— a peaceful, green place."

A stranger? No.

A foreigner? No—an American.

A spy?

Never!

Of Japanese ancestry? Yes, "But only Grove and I know about that."

A good, gentle man? Yes.

And the Sunday mornings of painting together and talking? What would happen to that?

His face seemed to appear before her: the deep, kind eyes—the color of the finest garden soil; the gentle smile; the clean-sunshine aroma of him.

And then Miss Ruth's mean face appeared and her bitter words sounded in Sophie's ears. *"You better stop spending time with that Chinaman of Anne's, right away!"*

"No, Miss Ruth. No," Sophie said aloud. "You sound like maybe we have something to hide, but we don't.

You make it sound *dirty*, but it isn't! We're simply friends, and I will not give up my friend!"

It isn't like that, Mama. He's a very nice man.

In the cottage at the back of Miss Anne's garden, Mr. Oto poured himself a cup of tea with hands that shook so badly, he almost spilled it.

What insanity! he was thinking. *A sneak attack? How dishonorable! How enraged the Americans will be—we will be! We are!*

And he wondered if Miss Anne was right about people in the town taking out their rage on *him*. Even if they all thought he was Chinese, not Japanese, wouldn't the sight of his oriental features be enough to send them into a rage?

The people of the town—how to tell what they would think or do. Because in the two years he had lived there, even though no one said anything unkind to him—except for Matilda, who was always somehow resentful toward him—he felt the chill behind their polite manners and their half-frozen smiles. And he also knew that even though he and Sophie could quietly meet to paint and talk on Sunday mornings, if they had been brazen enough to walk down the street together, even the half-frozen, smallest of smiles would stop, and the eyes would be hostile and accusing. That is, unless he walked behind her and carried her packages, as if he were a servant.

My dear Sophie! What is to become of our friendship now?

And the full grief came upon him at that moment. The loss would be unbearable!

But what am I thinking? Here will be war, and all I can think about is losing the Sunday mornings with my beloved. What kind of a man does that?

Chapter Twelve

*M*iss Anne said:

Oh, it was a terrible thing, I tell you! The whole world turned upside down, it seemed like, so that the little things I had been worried about—like making sure Mr. Oto planted the pink dogwoods in a straight row—suddenly seemed completely unimportant.

And another thing: The weather had turned unseasonably warm—made me feel like the whole world was getting ready to explode!

Our town was in such a state of shock—the whole country as well, I guess. But we didn't know about all of that yet.

Because back then, we didn't have television or anything like that, so all we had was the radio, mostly.

A couple of days after that terrible attack on Pearl Harbor, Mr. Johnson—he owned the drug store—started getting his clerk to drive all the way to Brunswick early every morning, to bring big-city newspapers back to Salty Creek. Because all we had was a weekly paper.

Every single day, folks were all lined up to buy those newspapers so they could read about the war.

And a war it certainly became—the very next day! President Roosevelt talked on the radio about the day that would "live in infamy," and later that same day, Congress declared that a state of war existed between the United States and Japan.

But the night of December seventh was one I would remember for the rest of my life—me making it through the late afternoon doing things that felt *normal*, but in such a complete silence.

I wound all the clocks in the house—the Seth Thomas mantel clock in the living room and the Regulator school clock in what had been the study—and yes, I still kept the study exactly as it had been the very day my husband passed on. And I took all the kitchen towels out of the deep drawer beside the sink and refolded all of them. At the last, I polished every single piece of silver in my whole house. Like maybe just wearing myself completely out would make me stop thinking about Pearl Harbor— and maybe about folks getting to hate that dear Mr. Oto for something he didn't have a blessed thing to do with— and get myself so tired out, I'd be able to sleep.

But no matter how hard I worked, worried feel- ings kept landing on me—like big buzzards fat, they could hardly fly at all.

Did I really know Mr. Oto?

Wasn't he, indeed, a foreigner?

Well, he certainly *looked* like one!

And all that bowing!

But in the next instant, all I could see was that freshly scrubbed *gentleman* taking tea at my very own table—his courteous manners, the clean-soap aroma of him, and those strong, brown hands holding one of my mama's teacups ever so carefully!

My Mr. Oto! An *American* man!

Well, I even drank a glass of warm milk before I went to bed—and how I do hate that! Still, I had to try everything I knew so I would be able to get some sleep.

But none of it worked. Because everything had changed—no denying that. So I went to bed but not to sleep. Instead, I decided that Mr. Oto would work only in the back of the house from now on, and whenever I had the chance, I would remind folks that he was Chinese, not Japanese! But then, I heard his gentle voice reminding me—and I sure did need reminding!—that he was an *American*.

A long, sleepless, terrible night it was.

The faucet in the bathroom dripped—*plunk . . . plunk . . . plunk.*

And a creaking sound in the hallway, like maybe a whole bunch of the enemy was coming to get me. And then the squawking of a strange-sounding and completely unfamiliar bird in my back garden.

Why, the beginnings of daylight were coming around the sides of my curtains before I finally fell asleep. But even then, it was a fitful sleep, full of blazing torches and white sheets and *fear*!

Chapter Thirteen

True to her word, Miss Anne forbade Mr. Oto to work in front of the house or to go anyplace where the people of the town would see him. Whenever they needed anything from town, Miss Anne sent Matilda or went herself. Mr. Oto remained out of sight.

The shock of the attack on Pearl Harbor and the war still seemed heavy on the town. Few people were out on the streets, but anyone walking along could hear the radios in almost every house—unseen voices droning out the terrible casualties America had endured—the USS *Arizona*, in particular, going down with over a thousand American souls lost.

Mr. Oto worked in the back garden v̶ ̶low, leisurely movements that belied the turmoil ̶ ̶ ing. And when the work was done, he spe̶ ̶ sitting in his hut, going deep inside hi̶ ̶ mine what he should do, if anything.

something was coming, that the people would eventually recover from their shock. And what they would feel would be a terrible, terrible outrage. What would they do with the outrage? That was the question. Oh, yes, that was certainly the question!

Would they form up a mob and come for him? And if they did, would they also come for Miss Anne, for harboring the *enemy*?

And what about Sophie?

At the thought of her name, an involuntary sob burst from his chest.

So that slowly, slowly, he began to understand what he must do. But first, he had to see his beloved Sophie— one last time.

So he endured the longest week of his entire life, and the next Sunday—exactly one week after Pearl Harbor—he went to the river, just as usual. But this time, he awakened very early, dressed in the dark before first light, and left for the river while night would still conceal him.

He had long hours to wait—if indeed, she came at all—but he was somehow strangely grateful for those hours. He sat by the river as quietly as the stump of a tree and breathed the day in and out, as light began untangling itself from the darkness. So that everything there was to see and to be with arose bit by bit out of the obscurity of night.

First the gray Spanish moss hanging from the branches of the live oak took on the wiry texture that separated it from the smooth, dark sky. And the line of saw grass across the river grew slowly distinct from the dark surface of the water. The sky itself slowly turned first a deep, rain-soaked gray and then pearl and finally, a soft and delicate rose. All of it so profound that Mr. Oto felt as if he were being reborn with the birth of the new day. And he was sure that Sophie would come to him there.

Finally, he began to sense her presence, almost as if he were willing her into being. He felt her walking toward him, even though he heard not a single footstep. So that when he turned his head slowly and she drifted into the edge of his vision, he was not surprised in the least.

He stood up and took a deep breath before he looked into her eyes—to see whatever was in them. And when he did look full into her face, all his concerns that she would think of him as the *enemy* vanished into the brilliant air. Because when she looked at him, there was no scorn, no anger, no bitterness—just a slightly bruised look about her, as if something deeply sad had entered her heart. So that he longed to take her into his arms, cradle her fine head on his shoulder, encase her with his body, so that nothing hurtful should ever come near her.

"I am so glad you have come," he finally managed to say.

Sophie took a sudden step toward him and then stopped. "I've been worried about you," she said in a clear, strong voice that rose above the bruised look of her eyes.

Mr. Oto touched the center of his chest. "*You* have been worried about *me?*"

"Why, yes!" She seemed surprised.

"Oh, but it is *I* who have been worried about *you!*" he stammered.

For a moment, they seemed close to laughing, but what was passing between them was far too serious for laughter.

"It's just that I haven't seen you since . . ."

"I know. Miss Anne thinks it's better for me not to be seen at all, right now."

"Oh."

Mr. Oto stared at the ground, thinking of what he knew was coming, and when he looked up again, Sophie was studying his face.

"What is it?" he whispered.

"I'm afraid for you, now that all this has happened. I'm afraid for you."

"Yes," he said simply. And then he added, "You shouldn't be seen with me."

"I know."

And the tone of her voice told him that there was already talk about Sophie and her friendship with a *foreigner*, a *Chinaman*, a lowly gardener.

"Has someone criticized you . . . because of me?" His concern for her was deep and most painful.

"Warned me," Sophie confessed, and then her cheeks flamed and a look of high resolve flashed in her eyes. "But the person who warned me is the same one who cost me my best friend when I was a little girl. I won't let her do that to me again!"

"I'm so sorry," he muttered.

"Oh, what's going to happen?" Sophie asked the question that she knew neither of them could answer.

"No one knows," he whispered. "No one knows where this will lead."

And for a brief moment, he wondered if they were speaking of the war at all, or perhaps speaking of themselves?

"It's already led to war!" Sophie spoke the last word with a shudder.

Mr. Oto let out a silent breath. For Sophie, theirs was only a friendship. For him, much more. But he must remain silent. So he quickly reminded himself that, at least, she still thought of him as her friend—despite Pearl Harbor.

"Yes, war again!" Sophie added.

The wound her words brought to him went very deep, and almost all the pain he felt was *her* pain. And another pain, as well—knowing that the leaders of his father's own country were responsible for this, her very visible grief.

And what can they be thinking, those leaders?

She spoke again, so suddenly that he was unprepared. "He was much taller than you," she said. "And I was very young and maybe even a little bit pretty. And he never came back."

"Who?" Mr. Oto whispered the word.

But she had turned away from him and was staring at the river, at the deep, black, ever-moving water. So that he stood silently, gazing at the plane of her back and with his hands hanging large and helpless by his sides.

But the urge he felt to comfort her was as unyielding as the certain surge of the river sliding past the banks, and as if in a dream, he moved toward her, both afraid of her strange grief and yet compelled to share it with her.

He stood directly behind her at last, with his hands coming up to touch her shoulders. But before he could do that, she turned to face him again, and she seemed not the least bit surprised to find him standing so close to her.

"Henry," she said. "I lost him in the war. World War One."

At first, he could say nothing. Nothing that he knew would help her. Then, "That is a very, very painful thing," he said. "I know, because I, too, lost someone." He heard his own voice, but until he heard the words, he didn't know what they would be.

"In the war?"

"No. Not in any war. But a loss nonetheless."

"I'm sorry to hear that," Sophie said.

"I lost the young woman who would have been my wife."

"And I lost the one who would have been . . . my husband," Sophie said, though her voice belied a complete conviction in the words. "The one I *believe* would have been my husband," she amended.

"Oh, he *would* have been," Mr. Oto said. "I'm sure of it."

His quiet pronouncement took her by surprise. But instantly, she knew that he was right. That's exactly what would have happened.

Yes. He would have been my husband.

It was so sweet a thought that when she looked again into Mr. Oto's deep eyes, she almost expected them to be Henry's eyes. Sparkling and blue and with silent laughter in them. But the eyes that looked back at her were the color of the black river. And just as fathomless.

"How did you lose her?" Sophie, too, did not know what the words would be until she heard them.

"She was from . . . my father's homeland," Mr. Oto said. "And she died of a fever on the ship, coming to this country. To marry me." He did not add, *And even in the midst of this madness of war, there could have been meaning to my life, because of her. But now, it is not her face I see. But yours.*

They never did get around to painting that day, but sat by the river together well into the early afternoon, sometimes speaking, but mostly just watching the river. A man and a woman who, at last, had shared their griefs and who were closer for the sharing. And two memories—one a tall young man with blazing blue eyes and unruly hair the color of the saw grass. The other a doll-size young woman wearing a richly embroidered red kimono.

When at last Sophie sighed, stood up, and brushed the grass from her skirt, he felt that he would die on the spot. But he was careful not to let his face show his agony.

"Promise me you will be careful," Sophie said, looking full into his eyes.

"I will be careful," he promised, bowing.

"And promise me that you'll come next Sunday," she added.

He hesitated for a moment, and then he said, "I will come, if I am able." And he did not add, *But I will not be able, for I will be protecting Miss Anne and you—my dear Sophie—in the only way I am able—by going far away.*

And the unspoken words tightened his throat.

Sophie nearly reached out to take his hand—not by design, but only because it seemed to be such a natural thing to do. But at the same instant, she shunned the impulse.

Mutely, Mr. Oto noticed the slight movement of her hand toward him and its immediate retreat. And he found it to be a completely endearing gesture that almost tore a sob from him.

He knew that their last Sunday together would be a memory for him to carry in his heart for the rest of his life. It glowed from his chest and radiated upward to his eyes, so that all the colors of the river and the trees and the sky seemed more brilliant than he had ever seen them before.

And her face in the center of all the colors. Her glorious, beautiful, wounded face!

So that when she turned and left, he watched her openly, watched as she turned and lifted a hand toward him before she disappeared.

He stayed by the river for a long time, and when at last he started to return to Miss Anne's house, he took a long and careful route, so that he would not be seen by any of the townspeople.

Sophie!

When Mr. Oto returned to his gardener's cottage that day, there was a sheet of paper in the seat of his chair. It had words scrawled on it: GO AWAY, DIRTY JAP!

Shaking, he tore up the paper; then he bathed thoroughly and dressed in his best clothes, before he walked across the garden toward Miss Anne's back door.

Chapter Fourteen

When Mr. Oto came up on the back porch, he noticed the gallon-size cans of begonias that he was to plant, and at the same time, he heard Miss Anne on the phone in her hallway.

"Of *course* he's Chinese," she was saying. "You don't think I would have him on my place if I thought he was one of *them*, do you? One of those Japs?"

In what was almost a dreamlike state, Mr. Oto stood on Miss Anne's porch, stunned and angered at the same time. Could this, then, be what the crane had come for? To remind him of his heritage? To warn him to protect Miss Anne?

"Yes, well I'll talk with you tomorrow," Miss Anne was saying into the receiver, and when he heard her hang up, he swallowed hard and knocked on the screen door.

When Miss Anne appeared, he could see most clearly the remnants of the overheard conversation still on her face. For even his dear Miss Anne looked at him differently than she had before Pearl Harbor. And now, knowing what he had to tell her—what he respected her far too much to withhold from her any longer—he felt his heart throbbing ominously beneath the clean shirt.

"You startled me!" Miss Anne said from the other side of the screen. "And where have you been, anyway? I told you to stay out of sight, and you've been gone somewhere almost all day long!"

"I know. I am sorry." Then he added, "Please, may I come in and speak with you?" He phrased his honest question so that, as he intended, she would be reminded of the full authority she had over whether or not he would be allowed to enter her house. Because, after all, everything was different now.

"Yes, come in," she said, after some hesitation. "I'm sorry. I have something on my mind."

"I know," he said as he entered the kitchen. He remained standing beside the sink while Miss Anne pulled out a chair from the table and sat down. Clearly preoccupied, she made no gesture for him to be seated.

"What is it you need to talk about?" she asked.

Now, it was his turn to hesitate. "I know that people are being critical of you for letting me stay here," he said.

Miss Anne looked up at him, surprised that he knew. "What I do is none of their business," she snapped, arguing more with herself than stating a fact.

"But I have deceived you," he said simply, and at his

words, Miss Anne stood, facing him squarely and with startled eyes.

"Exactly how have you deceived me, Mr. Oto?" Her voice was low and there was a faint glitter of something like fear in her eyes. *Dear God,* she was thinking, *Do I know this man? Do I really know him?*

"My family . . . ," he began, "My family is not from China, as I have allowed you to believe."

"Where are they from?"

"They are all in California, as I told you. But my father—long ago—came to this country from Japan."

"You're Japanese?" her eyebrows shot up in alarm.

"No, Miss Anne," he said in a soothing tone. "I am American. I was born in this country."

"But your people came from Japan?"

"My father came from Japan. That is true."

"Then why did you go on letting everyone think you were Chinese?"

"I never said that, Miss Anne." His tone was only slightly defensive.

"But *I* did, and you didn't bother to correct me," she argued.

"I apologize for that, " Mr. Oto said simply. "I didn't want to talk about my past, as that may have led to more questions than I was prepared to answer." And before he could stop himself, he bowed.

"Stop that!" Miss Anne spoke to him in a tone she had never used with him before. "I can't believe it!" she muttered, and sank back into the chair. "You . . . Japanese! One of them!"

"No, Miss Anne," he persisted. "I am American. I am just as American as you are."

At that, he drew her full rage. "As American as *I* am?" she sputtered. "I'll have you know that I am a member of the DAR!" But his puzzled expression told her that he didn't know what that meant.

"The Daughters of the American Revolution." She released the words like cannonballs. "That means that I am descended from a true patriot who fought for the independence of this country. Fought against England for it."

"That is very honorable, Miss Anne," he said.

"Are you making fun of me?" she shot back at him.

"No, Miss Anne," Mr. Oto protested quickly. "I meant only the greatest respect for you and for your ancestor. I have never spoken to you with anything but respect, and respect is all I mean now."

She studied him for a long moment. "That's true, what you say," she finally conceded. "You have never spoken to me except with respect."

"I am the same man now," he said carefully, "as I was before Pearl Harbor."

"But you are Japanese?" she questioned.

"No, Miss Anne," he answered in the same gentle voice. "American."

"What about your father?"

"My father is my father," he said simply. "I do not know anything about war. And I do not know anything about politics. I know only about flowers. And about friends."

"This is terrible," Miss Anne said, as if she were speaking only to herself. Then she looked at him intently. "What will happen if people find out?"

"I know that some already suspect it, and I am very afraid—for you."

"Afraid for me?" she asked incredulously. "Why on earth would you be afraid for me?"

"People in the town will blame you. There are some who think I am not Chinese, and they will not stop until they cause trouble more for you than for me. I can always go away to another place. But you must live here." *And,* he was thinking, *Sophie must live here also.* And he must not hurt her, no matter what the cost to himself.

"I must go away," he said. "Back to my family. And I must go now, before I cause trouble for you."

"No!" Miss Anne's voice was emphatic. Still, she recognized some wisdom in what Mr. Oto said. For after all, she would, indeed, be severely ostracized . . . perhaps even called a traitor—*Dear Lord!*—for harboring a Japanese, even if he was an American.

"Please do not worry," Mr. Oto said. "I will find a way to get there."

Long minutes of silence then, with Miss Anne looking at Mr. Oto while he gazed at his shoes. Maybe it would be better to do as he had done before—get on a bus and go away. To protect Miss Anne. Then she could honestly say that he was gone.

But would taking a bus still be possible? Only two years ago, people merely regarded him with a mild interest. Now, he would attract deep suspicion and maybe even open hatred. For although he was an American, his face and his body bore the image of the Enemy.

Miss Anne's voice interrupted his thinking. "You can't go away," she said simply. "I can't bear not knowing what has happened to you." Then she paused and cleared her throat. "And besides, you'd attract too much attention. We'll have to hide you, that's what we'll do. Tell everyone you've gone far away . . . Canada, maybe. Yes. Tell them you have family in Canada, and you are Chinese. That will do it. For both of us," she added. "That way, I can say you're gone—and it will be the truth."

Mr. Oto knew instantly that she was right. It was the only way to save them both, but especially to save her. For if he were arrested, word could somehow get back to Salty Creek, and Miss Anne would be called an enemy sympathizer, even if no one had found the letter he wrote to his father.

Miss Anne was right. Hiding was the only answer for them. But where?

"You know, I may just have an answer," Miss Anne said, as if she had looked into his mind and seen the question. "Long years ago, my papa had a fishing cabin about three miles below the salt marsh. It's way back in the brush, and I own the property, so I know no one's been using it. That would be a place where we could hide you and no one would ever know. We'll have to be careful, of course."

"We." Mr. Oto whispered the word.

"*We,*" Miss Anne said emphatically.

Miss Anne had been struck with two simple statements he had made to her: first and foremost, that he was an American; and, too, that he was the same man that day as he had been for the two years he had lived in her gardener's cottage and worked for her.

So that settled it, as far as she was concerned, and she stood up. "You go gather your things, and I'll put some canned goods and bottles of drinking water in a box—there isn't any fresh water down there. We'll leave before dawn, so no one will see us go. And . . ."—Miss Anne was clearly rising almost happily to the challenge of the task before her—"I'll drive on over to Brunswick right after I drop you off at Papa's cabin. That way, when people ask, I can tell them that I took you over there to catch a more direct bus to Canada."

"If anyone asks," Mr. Oto added, "tell them you made me leave because I was a Jap." His tongue almost faltered on the word. "That will help to protect you, and you and I will know the truth."

Chapter Fifteen

*M*iss Anne said:

I wondered what on earth the world was coming to, when a good, solid *American* man like my Mr. Oto had to be hidden away like a criminal. But on the other hand, his father certainly was Japanese, no getting away from that!

I watched him walk away, out onto my back porch, and I saw him glance at the begonias waiting to be planted. He looked at them for a long time before he went on down the steps and across the back garden.

Put an awful catch in my throat, that did!

And maybe that's when I realized just how many Americans had been so deeply hurt by that Sunday that would "live in infamy." All those fine young men killed, without any warning! And all those other Americans—like dear Mr. Oto—suffering, too.

And me! Yes, me suffering as well.

Why, I always thought that as they got older, ladies

were supposed to have peace, at least. But my peaceful days were already over, even though I didn't know it.

So that Sunday evening, only a week to the day after Pearl Harbor, I went about gathering all the things Mr. Oto would need to take with him, and I felt almost like a spy, myself!

And what about the lie I was going to have to tell, once somebody—anybody—asked me about where Mr. Oto had gone off to?

Why, I'd never told a lie in my whole life! At least, not really. Only little white lies to keep from hurting folks' feelings. Like the time Ruth brought back that ridiculous, ugly hat from her shopping trip to Brunswick and wore it all the time. When nobody said anything about it—trying to be polite, you see—she got to where she'd come right out and *ask*!

"Why, I think it's . . . fine!" I said, when Ruth nailed me about it.

That kind of little white lie. Sure were lots of us had to do that about Ruth's hat.

But an out-and-out, bald-faced *lie*?

Never!

At least, never before.

Chapter Sixteen

That night, Mr. Oto never went to sleep at all, but he gathered his few items of clothing—most of them still filled with the crisp aroma of sunshine from hanging on the clothesline, carefully rolled up the watercolor portrait of Sophie as the Crane-Wife, and placed it safely in the small suitcase the doctor's wife had sent with him when he first came to live in the cottage.

Afterward, he sat on the cot and tried to imagine exactly what the hour was by the movement of the ghostly finger of silver moonlight across his floor. At around two in the morning, he heard the back gate to the garden squeak ever so slightly, and before Miss Anne could even knock on his door, he was up and ready to leave.

They tiptoed back across the garden together, and he realized then that perhaps he would not work with the flowers again. How sad to be sneaking away like a thief in the night and leaving the plants he had tended so lovingly. And leaving Sophie. Leaving her to the silent might-have-beens.

How can I bear it?

Under the dark porte cochere, they entered Miss Anne's car noiselessly, not even daring to close the doors until after she had backed out of the driveway and they had gone several blocks down the street.

"Did you remember to bring that old tarpaulin?" she asked into the darkness. "No telling what condition the roof is in, and you may need it to keep the rain off yourself."

"I remembered," Mr. Oto said.

"And how about that liniment you use on your knees?" she asked.

"I remembered," Mr. Oto repeated, wondering to himself how Miss Anne knew about that.

After that, Miss Anne said nothing more, and they drove in silence out beyond the end of town and down the same sandy road he and Sophie had walked on for the past Sunday mornings. When they passed that place where Mr. Oto knew the giant live oak was standing, his throat tightened.

"Now don't you worry about a thing," Miss Anne said, as if she could feel his sadness. "I'm sure people will come to their senses soon and realize that Americans are Americans . . . no matter where their families came from before they came here."

But, of course, that wasn't what was making Mr. Oto sad, and so once again, he felt guilty. How could it be that at a time when so many other things should be on his mind, his only thought was of Sophie? And what about her? What would happen when she heard, as everyone else would hear, about his going away to Canada? Would she care?

On they drove, until, not more than two miles beyond the live oak tree, Miss Anne stopped the car and peered ahead of her into the darkness while the idling engine hummed quietly.

"It's been a long time. I hope I can still find it. Used to be a big palm tree around here, and right on the other side of it was a little trail led off through the palmettos—not much more than a path, even that long ago. By now, it might be all grown over."

She shifted the gears and the car lumbered ahead, its blazing headlights cutting through the darkness to reveal increasingly thick undergrowth on either side of the narrow road. Then, another half-mile farther on, she stopped again.

"This has to be it," she said, as if she were arguing with herself. "Shine the flashlight over there." She directed Mr. Oto's attention to the far side of the road. Sure enough, the beam of light pointed out a thin, sandy trail that led off into the underbrush. Still, he did not move, but sat silently until Miss Anne spoke.

"You go on ahead now, Mr. Oto. And be careful where you're stepping. I'll come back on Sunday night and leave more groceries for you right on the other side of that palm tree, where nothing will be visible if anyone comes along the road."

"And," she added, "anything special you need, you

just write it down on a piece of paper and stick it right in that same place."

"Thank you," he said, and as quickly as he could, he got out of the car, ran across the road in the glare of the headlights, and shone the flashlight beam toward the trail. Then he turned and waved at Miss Anne before he went off through the palmettos, following a thin, overgrown path. Behind him in the darkness, he heard the grinding of gears as Miss Anne turned around and headed back toward town, where he knew she would take the turn in the road that would lead her all the way to Brunswick. And just for him.

Then there was nothing but silence, the sound of his feet in the sand, and his own breathing.

In the darkness and the silence that was broken only by the beam of the flashlight and by faint and mysterious scurrying in the underbrush, he moved forward along the sandy path, only occasionally raising the beam of the light to try and penetrate the velvet darkness ahead of him, throwing into relief palmetto fronds that tangled together like interwoven fingers and higher up, gray moss-beards in the trees—old Spanish ghosts waiting to drop onto him, to press him into the sand and chuckle triumphantly, "The enemy!"

On and on, deeper and deeper into the brush, until he began wondering if perhaps Miss Anne had been wrong about how far it was from the road to the cabin. Worse, perhaps the cabin wasn't even there anymore, had fallen in upon itself long years ago. Or maybe it had never been there at all.

And what would happen to him if that were true, he wondered. Daylight would come, eventually, after he had walked all night trying to find a place that didn't even exist, and he would have to find someplace to hide, where he could wait until the dark came again and then . . . what? Go back to Miss Anne's house in town? No. He couldn't endanger her by going back. Besides, by tomorrow, she probably would have started telling people that he had gone to Canada. Would have lied for him.

No. This time I will not dishonor those who have trusted me.

As if in confirmation of his resolve, the sand became firmer under his feet, and slowly, the palmettos thinned, the scrub pines grew taller, and he could smell the river somewhere ahead of him, the fertile-sour aroma of black mud alive with fiddler crabs.

When he shone the flashlight beam ahead of him once more, its long finger of light barely touched the weathered side of a small shack built up on concrete blocks near a grove of live oak trees hung with moss. A shack that blended in with the gray trees and the gray moss almost completely. Miss Anne was right. It was completely concealed and far away from where anyone would come to fish in the river. With a feeling that was a mixture of elation and of a certain sadness, Mr. Oto had to admit that no one—other than Miss Anne, of course—would ever know where he had gone.

As it turned out, Matilda was the first one to ask Miss Anne about it, of course.

"Where's your Chinaman gone off to?" she demanded of Miss Anne in her typical straightforward manner only a few hours after Miss Anne had returned from her early—and solitary—drive to Brunswick and back.

"Why, he's gone to Canada," Miss Anne answered quickly, and she silently berated herself for not even thinking about Matilda and how she would notice— right away—any change in the household or the routine of the days. But as far as people in the town were concerned, Miss Anne knew that Mr. Oto had always been so quiet and unobtrusive, it would be a few days before anyone noticed he was gone. Miss Anne had been depending upon a few days of respite before she had to start telling the lie. But she had forgotten about Matilda.

"Good riddance!" Matilda bellowed, startling Miss Anne out of her thinking. "Didn't like that Chinaman one little bit. No, ma'am, not one little bit!"

Matilda said nothing more and neither did Miss Anne, but later in the morning, when Miss Anne passed through the kitchen, she heard Matilda slamming the iron down hard against the ironing board and muttering, "Canada . . . humph!"

Sophie made herself wait until Wednesday before she walked past Miss Anne's house, hoping to see Mr. Oto working in the garden. Of course, she knew that Miss Anne was trying to keep him out of sight. He had told her that much himself. But still, she hoped to catch a glimpse of him and didn't wonder to ask herself why. And when she couldn't find him anywhere, a feeling of disappointment crept over her, as if the sun had suddenly gone behind a cloud.

"But Miss Anne is wise," Sophie whispered to herself as she went on down the sidewalk. "She is protecting him. And he probably *needs* protection, right now, at least. So I know he's safe, and that's all I need to know. Besides, I'll see him on Sunday. He promised he would come!"

And in that way, Sophie comforted herself.

She tried her best to stay busy, but that next week turned out to be the longest week of her entire life.

When she tended her crab traps, the mere perfume of the salt marsh brought with it the crisp aroma of his spanking-clean shirt, and when she worked in her garden, it was *his* strong, brown fingers that tended the plants so carefully. The poetry she read aloud arrived in her ears bearing his precise, gentle voice.

On Saturday, when she went to the hardware store to buy lightbulbs, *he* seemed to be standing beside her, holding a packet of pink petunia seeds and smiling. So she bought lightbulbs, but she also bought a new packet of pink petunia seeds, which she propped against the sugar bowl on her kitchen table.

And finally, when Sunday came, she was awake long before daylight. So that in the quiet warmth of her own kitchen, she sipped her tea gratefully and studied the seed packet with joy.

As soon as the sky had turned a bright gray, she started for the river. On the way, she plucked a small twig of baby-pink bougainvillea and carried it along until she reached the sanctuary of the riverbank. Then she stuck the sprig of flowers into her hair.

Because she had arrived so early, the river still held the last remnants of the night, with the light pale and uncertain, wavering through the trees in milky glimmers. And the face of the river was uncommonly smooth, so that she placed her paper and paints in the chair and walked to its very edge.

Across the expanse of smooth, silver water, the seemingly unending sea of golden saw grass, with the blades barely distinguishable in the early light, and far up the river, a massive live oak that arose from the golden grasses and in whose slate-gray branches perched a multitude of snowy egrets, like white candles in a twilight cathedral.

Near her, a quick swishing sound in the water, where a fish briefly rippled the surface, and then she looked down at her own reflection in the ever-enlarging rings on the disturbed surface. Her dark brows undulating in the moving water and the pink flower in her hair like a wavering, pink sun arising over her left ear. Behind her, Mr. Oto's face appeared, the gentle eyes and the Botticelli-cherub smile so delightfully misplaced in the broad, oriental face.

She turned, but he was not there. Only the silence and shadows all around her.

She even tried, then, to start her painting, thinking that once again, she would attempt capturing the distinct characteristics of the sky over where the river and the ocean came together, but her mind refused to take seriously any of the lines or the colors she anticipated putting on the paper. Instead, only his face moved before her, gently undulating as if it were reflected in the deep, dark water of the slow-moving river.

The long minutes dragged by—becoming decidedly less lovely because he was not there. The minutes became hours.

"Grove?" she whispered to the empty riverbank. "Grove? Where are you?"

Then the fear began to descend upon her. What if something had happened to him? But wouldn't she have known? Such a small town can't keep many secrets. If something had happened to him, Miss Anne would have told her. She was sure of it.

Finally, she gathered her unopened paints and packed away the still pristine paper and wondered what had happened. He promised to come . . . and then she remembered the condition upon which he made the promise: "if I am able."

Perhaps he was ill?

On her way back home, she walked slowly, thinking about how to find out what was wrong, and she remembered to remove the sprig of bougainvillea from her hair before she passed through town. She put it carefully into her pocket and wondered yet again where he could be. Because his not coming was more than just that.

Somehow, it was much more.

Chapter Seventeen

By Monday, she could think of nothing else.

Get hold of yourself, Sophie! she admonished in a silent voice that sounded strangely like her mother's voice. *You're acting like a child! You must remember to act like a lady!*

No ma'am, Mama, another part of her responded. *Not like a child. And not like a lady, either. Like a woman.*

So that the whole day, the voices argued within her. And all the while, the sprig of pink bougainvillea wilted quietly on her dresser.

Finally, she decided that perhaps she would just make a call on Miss Anne. That would certainly be nothing new, though she hadn't been to see her old friend in several weeks. But in that way, she could ask about Mr. Oto right in the course of casual conversation. Still, she finally rejected that idea, because she felt certain that Miss Anne would notice that her inquiries about Mr. Oto, no matter how lightly phrased, were more than just polite conversation. Especially if Sophie were right there in Miss Anne's own parlor, seated in a chair and maybe with her hands making the cup clatter against the saucer. Miss Anne knew her far too well. Miss Anne would know right away, and then what would Sophie do? Confess? Confess *what?* That she cared very much about him? And what would her old friend say to that? Her own gardener!

On Tuesday morning, as she walked toward the library, Sophie saw Miss Anne herself digging among the marigolds Mr. Oto had planted and tended so carefully. And she hesitated only for a moment before she stopped by the fence and called out, "Miss Anne? Is Mr. Oto ill?" She did everything she could do to keep her voice light and sound casual, but still, it held a faint tremor that would not have been lost on Miss Anne one bit, if Miss Anne hadn't been rather startled by the fact that once again, she was facing the telling of the big lie.

And who would have thought it would be so hard? And especially, having to lie to Sophie!

Miss Anne came to the fence, all the while looking at the handful of weeds she had pulled from the flower beds, as if they were the only thing in the world worthy of her interest.

"Mr. Oto has gone to Canada," she said matter-of-factly. "To be with his family," she added, still studying the handful of weeds.

"Oh." It was a small utterance from Sophie, but the way she said it surprised Miss Anne somehow——she couldn't have said exactly *how.* But she wondered briefly why the word seemed to be wreathed in a sigh of the smallest magnitude.

Sophie, on second thought, noticed that Miss Anne didn't look at her when she spoke of Mr. Oto. Why was her old friend acting so distant and cool about it? For after all, Miss Anne had never made a secret about her genuine fondness for him. But somehow, everything about Miss Anne felt different now to Sophie. Of course, Sophie would never pry, but she couldn't help wonder about it. What on earth was wrong? And how could she possibly ask Miss Anne more about him?

She couldn't, that's all. So they stood there, the two old friends, separated by a white, picket fence and by a silence that neither of them could fill.

"Well," Sophie said at last. "I'm sure you'll miss him. He always took such good care of your garden. You need for me to bring you anything from the store?"

Mama was right, Sophie was thinking. *Nothing lasts.*

Miss Anne's strange aloofness seemed to relax a little. "I'll certainly miss him," she agreed, still studying the weeds, "And no, thank you—I'll be going to the store a little later myself. But I appreciate it."

Sophie moved on a little down the sidewalk, wishing that there were some way of asking the questions she wanted to ask—but there wasn't. It was just that simple. Finally, she just waved her hand and walked on. But she could feel Miss Anne's eyes upon her as she walked away, and her gait felt awkward and unnatural, so she raised her arm and studied her watch, as if she were late for an appointment.

And indeed, Sophie's feelings were accurate, for Miss Anne still stood at the fence, watching her walk away down the sidewalk.

My, Miss Anne thought, *she certainly looks pretty this morning, but I can't quite put my finger on what it is.* She lingered for yet another moment, wincing at the feeling of isolation wrought by the telling of the lie. *Sophie! I want so very much to tell you. But I can't involve you in this. It's far too serious.*

At the cabin, Mr. Oto had settled in as well as he was able, doing everything exactly as Miss Anne directed him. He had torn a blanket apart and tacked the pieces over the windows and over the doorway, so the light from the kerosene lamp couldn't be seen at night. He never went out during the daylight, and he carefully buried his empty cans in among the palmetto bushes, away from the faint path.

He propped up his painting of the Crane-Wife on a small, wooden box against the wall and even gathered a few mature stalks of golden dune-grass, which he placed on the floor in front of the painting—almost like a shrine before which he spent long hours in meditation.

It was a time of surprising and profound grief for him. And shame. Shame that the deepest grief in him was not for his father and his brothers, their wives and sons and grandsons, not even for the war—terrible war. But for the loss of those precious hours with Sophie, a loss that was a thousand times more painful than he had ever anticipated. His mind returned over and over to every moment they had spent together on the river-bank, so that in his memory, he walked along a strand of silken thought that occasionally held a perfectly round, luminous pearl. Her face in one, her laughter on another, her pale arms in the morning light, her deep green eyes. And finally, her soul's hunger for that dome of sky over where the river and the ocean came together.

Finally, without even a flashlight to guide him—for he feared that the beam would be seen by someone—he walked one dark night all the way back to the big live oak tree, to that place where he and Sophie had been together on those glorious Sunday mornings, and there, he sat in Sophie's chair, trying to draw her presence forth and to wear it on his body like another skin. He fancied that he could breathe her perfume and that somehow the chair still held the warmth of her. So he stayed in her presence until the dawn was coming fast, and he had to hurry to get back to the shack, where he slept deeply and peacefully until almost noon.

Later that day, a breeze lifted out the blanket over the window and allowed the bright light of day to fall upon his sleeping face. He sat up, groggy and a little con-fused, wondering what time it was and what day it was and what seemed to be calling to him.

Cautiously, he stuck his head out through the blan-keted doorway, and the glare of a totally clear day made him rub his eyes and the earth was so hushed and still that he wondered for a moment if his hearing had sud-denly gone bad. Like watching a silent movie, he saw the palmetto bushes and the gray-beard moss hanging motionlessly.

And the great crane standing at the base of the largest live oak tree, its white feathers like a mound of sunlit snow against the gnarled shades of moss and old velvet. It turned its head just the least little bit, to gaze at him full in the face.

"Sophie?" he whispered, as if it were the only word he could find to utter.

But the crane did not even blink its eyes at the sound of his voice, and so Mr. Oto and the crane stood, gazing at each other for long, silent minutes, until Mr. Oto blinked in the glare, and when he looked again, it was gone.

On the next Sunday night, he walked back to the road—during darkness, of course—to find a cardboard box with supplies in it, left by Miss Anne, as she had promised. Canned goods and more kerosene for the lamp, a big box of matches wrapped in waxed paper, and clean, dry clothes that still smelled of the musty closet and that must have belonged to Miss Anne's long-deceased father. And the weekly newspaper that came out every Thursday afternoon, so that he read every word of it over and over again, especially about the war. And the shaking of his hands echoed the flickering flame in the kerosene lantern.

Chapter Eighteen

*M*iss Anne said:

Lordy, it was a hard time, sure enough. Maybe people today, who don't really know anything about Pearl Harbor, don't know what a terrible thing it was. Folks were all incensed about it. And scared, to boot. Makes for a bad combination, that does. And everybody looking at the newsreels at the theater in Brunswick, showing those goose-stepping Nazis—enough to curdle the blood, it was. And then showing all those Japs lined up in front of their planes and throwing up their arms in the air all at the same time and screaming in unison. And wanting nothing more than to kill us.

And you know, I thought that telling the lie about Mr. Oto would get easier, but it didn't. Deep in my heart, I knew there wasn't one thing wrong with what I was doing to help a fellow American. But the strain of it was much more than I'd expected, and one day, when I went to the post office and saw that big poster of Uncle

Sam looking so stern and serious, pointing his finger and saying "I want YOU!" I just about jumped out of my skin. Because no matter how right I was, I still felt funny about it. Way deep inside. And so very much alone with it. Carrying the secret around all by myself. It was hard!

When I finally ran into Ruth in the grocery store, it was quite a difficult thing. She'd always been such a busybody, and I had dreaded seeing her. Not that she was ever evil—or even downright mean—or anything like that. Why, in over thirty years, she never missed so much as one single Sunday of church. Or so she said, at least. But I was enough like my papa to know that churchgoing doesn't guarantee goodness in anyone. And Ruth certainly had a way of enjoying bad news. Or something like that. And wouldn't you know, she lit right in on me about Mr. Oto.

"Anne!" she yelled at me that day, and before I could even turn around all the way, she jammed her buggy right up alongside me and looked at me so hard with those bright little eyes—always did look like she was getting ready to say *Ah-hah! Gotcha!*

"I've been wanting to ask you about that foreign man of yours," she said. Well, she always did know how to get right at the heart of what she wanted to know. No polite chitchat for her, sure enough, just blunt and open questions without any warm-up whatsoever. I don't mean to speak ill of the dead, so God rest her soul, I guess.

"I hear he's gone away?" she framed it as a question, but it was a statement if ever I heard one. I tossed two boxes of Jell-O into my buggy and tried the best I could to look absolutely unconcerned. I also made a quick mental note not to buy some things I'd been planning on getting for Mr. Oto—more matches and several cans of beans. Such as that.

"Yes, he's gone," I said, looking back up at the shelves and reaching out to take down a box of cornstarch, though I still had half a box in my pantry.

"Where'd he go?" she asked.

"Went back to his family in Canada," I answered, tossing the unneeded box of cornstarch on top of the Jell-O.

"Canada?" She said it as if she had never heard of such a thing.

"That's right." I picked up a box of unflavored gelatin, which was simply the next thing I saw along the shelf.

"Well, I expect you're going to miss him," she said. "He sure did leave sudden-like."

"Yes." I tossed the unflavored gelatin into the buggy. "My garden will certainly never be as lovely as it was when I had him around to take care of it." *There!* I thought. *How wonderful it feels to say something that's absolutely true!*

The rest of her comment, I decided to ignore.

"Well, to tell you the truth, your garden wasn't the only thing he was interested in," she said in a voice that dared me to ignore that deep pronouncement. I turned to look at her for the first time.

Might as well, I supposed—or I was going to wind up with a buggy full of things I didn't need or want.

"Beg pardon?" I pretended that I hadn't quite heard her.

She leaned close to me and whispered, "I said your garden wasn't the only thing he was interested in." Her brittle little eyes sparkled behind the thick glasses. "He was interested in Sophie, too, so I hear."

Sophie? What on earth could she mean? I knew I had to be careful, because getting taken by surprise like that was likely to make me mess up the story I had rehearsed so carefully.

"Sophie? What do you mean?" I asked.

"Just that he's been meeting her every Sunday morning down by the river—them all alone like that while decent folks are in church. Why, she hasn't been to services in almost two months—and all because of him. And you didn't know anything about that?"

"Why, no." I didn't know what else to add, and what I really wanted to do was walk right away from her, but to be truthful, I was too curious to do that. Because after all, I thought I had noticed something or other in Sophie's voice when I told her about him going off to Canada, and I'd been wondering and wondering about it ever since. But still, it just didn't make a bit of sense. *Sophie and Mr. Oto? How ridiculous!*

"They met every single Sunday morning . . . alone," Miss Ruth hissed.

"What for?" I asked, not thinking too clearly.

"Supposed to be painting pictures, so I hear. But I think it was something more than that. And you know, of course, that she's always been a little wild. But she's got to be just as crazy as her Aunt Minnie to get mixed up like that with such a *dark* man. And a foreigner to

· 129 ·

boot! Especially these days, with us not knowing who's a spy and who's not!"

Of course, I knew that Sophie liked to paint watercolors of the river, and I also knew that Mr. Oto sometimes did artwork, but I never thought about the two of them together. And what was that Miss Ruth was saying about spies, anyway?

"Spies?" I felt something hot and alarmed creeping up the back of my neck.

"Well," Miss Ruth laughed. "You just don't keep up with the news like you used to, do you? There was a rubber raft found on South Beach yesterday—and it all cut to ribbons and half buried in the sand. Sheriff thinks some spies came off a submarine in it."

"But what does that have to do with Sophie?"

"Nothing . . . maybe. Except that maybe that Mr. Oto of yours was a spy, too. A Japanese spy pretending to be a Chinaman. But now the German spies have come, he could go on to a new assignment in Canada."

"But he *was* Chinese," I protested.

"So he said," Miss Ruth shot back at me. "But who's to know for sure?" Then she lowered her voice into a conspiratorial whisper, "She's done it before, you know—had an affair."

"Why, Ruth! You're just as wrong as wrong can be!" I rebutted her cruel words. "And besides, he's gone now, anyway." I spoke a little more softly—because after all, I didn't want to protest too much, as they say. So I took down a package of paper muffin cups from the shelf and tossed it on top of the unflavored gelatin and the cornstarch and the Jell-O. Then I gripped the handle of the buggy tightly and marched ahead.

Ruth didn't follow me, but in a couple of seconds, she called out from behind me, "What kind of recipe you using that calls for Jell-O *and* unsweetened gelatin? Better be careful! You'll never be able to get your teeth through it, whatever it is!"

All in all, I thought Ruth was quite crude in her gossiping, and maybe that's what was on my mind more than wondering what on earth had been going on—if anything—between Mr. Oto and Sophie. And wondering why they would have been meeting like that. Still, that would certainly explain Sophie's thinly veiled disappointment when I told her that he had gone to Canada.

But I knew Sophie very, very well. And Mr. Oto, too—and I also knew with no doubt whatsoever that he was a true gentleman and that she was a true lady. So even if they were meeting, it was just as friends. Nothing more. I was sure of it. And I certainly hated knowing that folks in town were talking about Sophie. I mean, if Ruth was saying something about it to me, then she had probably already spread it all over town. Sophie was a real lady, and I didn't like her being the subject of such gossip, especially the crude way Ruth put it.

Poor old Ruth—she's been gone now a long time. She got real senile in her later years, but not quite the way Sophie's old Aunt Minnie did—by living in the past—but by getting downright dirty-minded about things. It was a strange thing to happen to her, but then we never really know how it's going to be for us when we get old, anyway.

I never did use all that unflavored gelatin or the cornstarch. Wish I'd bought extra sugar, though, instead of those things, because it wasn't too long after that when we all had to start using rations for sugar and for meat . . . even for gasoline. Because of the war.

Well, that was on Friday when Ruth said those things to me, and the next Sunday night was the last time I took supplies to Mr. Oto. Because everything started going wrong about then, starting out when Matilda called me late Sunday afternoon and said she wouldn't be coming to work that week. In fact, that she didn't know when she would be back at all.

"There's a bad storm coming," she announced to me on the phone, using that solemn-pronouncement tone I knew so well. The same tone she used whenever she was sure that her cake would fail because the eggs weren't fresh enough or that we were going to have rain by afternoon because her knees were aching. Funny thing was, she was usually right.

"Big storms don't come this late and when the weather's this cool," I argued, though I knew, even then, that I may as well save my breath.

"Well, *this* one's coming, sure enough. And before the next full moon," she assured me. "And I'm taking my children and going to my mama's over in Waycross. Inland. Away from the ocean. It's gone be a bad one. You better take care, Miss Anne."

With that dire warning, she hung up, leaving me feeling strangely vulnerable and afraid.

Chapter Nineteen

*M*iss Anne said:

That last Sunday night that I took supplies to the big palm tree for Mr. Oto, he was crouching behind the tree, waiting for me.

Nearly scared me to death, he did, popping out of the dark like that at me, and of course, the fact that he had startled me led to all kinds of apologies and bows.

"I thought you were going to stop that," I snapped at him, though really, it was my being startled that made me angry.

"I'm sorry," he said, and bowed again. Honestly, he was just hopeless.

"What are you doing here, anyway?" I asked, glancing up and down the road. Because anyone who happened to come along couldn't help but notice us there, what with my car barely pulled off the road. And us right out in the middle of nowhere like that.

"What's going to happen, Miss Anne?" he asked, and

I really didn't know what he meant by it. And besides, I was intent on getting back home before someone saw us, so I certainly didn't want to stand there and carry on a conversation with him.

"Happen?" It was the only thing I could utter.

"Yes. What will happen to us if someone finds out?"

Well, that was the very last thing in the world I wanted to talk about, because it scared me to death. And like I said, when I get scared, I get angry. Always have. Always will.

"Don't ask!" I snapped at him. "Just don't ask."

And even in the bare light created by the headlights of the car, I could see that his face bore all the proof of his concern. He was very drawn-looking and worn, as if he were grieving.

"No one will find out," I said, wanting to do or say anything I could to smooth the worried look in his face.

"What you are doing for me . . ." he started, but his voice trailed off, so whatever else he would have said, I never knew.

"I'm only doing what has to be done," I said. "And I'm doing it for an American. That's all that matters."

For a few seconds, neither of us said anything else, and I believe the words had comforted both of us. Soothed my conscience quite a bit, that's for sure. But strangely, those very words that soothed me turned around and made me mad as fire all over again! And maybe part of that was the mere thought that any native-born American should have to be afraid! Right here in his own country!

"What if someone finds me here? And what if they accuse you of harboring the enemy?" The voice was still soft, but plaintive.

"No one will find you," I said, but I certainly didn't feel all that confident that I was right. Somehow, Ruth's glittering eyes seemed to manifest themselves out of the headlights' gleam.

And that thought scared me so bad that I just shoved the box of canned goods and bottles of fresh water into Mr. Oto's hands and went and got in my car and drove away.

Left him standing there in the dark. And that was the last time I ever saw him.

Chapter Twenty

On the following Sunday, Sophie went to church for the first time since she'd begun painting at the riverbank with Mr. Oto, because she couldn't bear the emptiness of the riverbank—and neither could she bear to stay at home, in the rooms where her mother's voice kept whispering, Nothing lasts.

Right on time, too, Miss Ruth noted, when Sophie came in. Now that heathen's gone. Bad enough, it was, Anne harboring an infidel. But for him to entice Sophie away from the Lord!

And she also noticed that Sophie was very pale and seemed to be distracted, in a strange kind of way. And that during the entire sermon, Sophie didn't listen to a word, but gazed through the window.

There's something, Miss Ruth thought, once again. I'm sure of it. It has to be more than painting!

For Sophie, the service seemed to go on forever, the sounds of the words lulling her, so that her eyes were drawn irresistibly to the window and beyond. To the green palm fronds and the blue sky. To the riverbank and the dank aroma of early morning. To the quiet sounds. The gentle whisper of the river sliding past the banks and the far-off calling of gulls.

So that the sudden chord of the last hymn shocked her thoughts, and she twitched at its sudden intrusion. It took her a moment or two to discover that she was completely accustomed to hearing the music from a distance, in soft and muted tones. And before she could stop herself, she glanced over at Miss Ruth and caught the briefest glimpse of the little eyes glittering behind the thick lenses.

The next week, Sophie passed by Miss Anne's house nearly every morning, and her steps always hesitated, as if she couldn't make up her mind whether to turn and go up the walkway or to keep on going.

On Thursday, her feet made up her mind for her, and as she walked between the borders of the marigolds, she could almost imagine Mr. Oto's strong hands working the soil around them. So that by the time she knocked on the front door, her heart was fluttering around inside her like a frightened bird.

When Miss Anne heard the knocking, her first thought was that it was Miss Ruth coming to pry. So that when she saw Sophie's face peering through the screened door, she felt almost faint with relief.

But when she opened the door and saw the lines in Sophie's face and the worn look in her eyes, she knew right away that something was wrong.

Of course, she thought. *Someone's told her about Ruth and the nasty gossip she's been spreading.*

And only after the two of them were settled in the big chairs by the front window did Miss Anne carefully start bringing up the topic of Sophie's obvious distress.

"Forgive me for saying so, Sophie," she began as kindly as possible. "But you're looking so tired, I'm worried about you."

Sophie smiled at that, and just the simple act of smiling seemed to bring a bit of color to her cheeks. Miss Anne sat back in her chair and felt a little less worried. After all, if Sophie could still smile, then perhaps she wasn't taking Ruth's gossiping all that seriously.

"I'm fine," Sophie said. "Just haven't been sleeping very well."

"I certainly know what that's like," Miss Anne agreed, and of course, she didn't add that she hadn't had a night of good, deep sleep since the attack on Pearl Harbor and the conflicts it had created in the most private recesses of her own soul.

"Miss Anne, why did Mr. Oto go off so suddenly?" The question was entirely unexpected and found Miss Anne unprepared to answer. She would have expected a question like that from Ruth, but not from Sophie. So that she stared at Sophie dumbly for several long moments before she could answer.

"It's just what he decided to do," she said finally.

"He didn't say why?"

Miss Anne noticed how carefully Sophie was speaking.

Obviously, Sophie was wondering if that terrible gossip had made the quiet and gentle Mr. Oto so miserable that he had to leave. "No, he didn't. It was just something he decided to do."

"Oh."

"But I know what's bothering you, Sophie," Miss Anne said in an entirely gentle voice.

"You do?" Sophie felt just as if she'd had an electric shock. Just what did her old friend know? And if worst came to worst and she suspected that Sophie truly had cared for Mr. Oto—beyond simple friendship—then she would know more than Sophie had been willing to admit, even to herself.

"Just don't pay any attention to her." Miss Anne was continuing, and Sophie struggled to catch up with what she was saying.

"Her?" What on earth was Miss Anne talking about?

"Miss Ruth, of course." But Miss Anne paused and looked at Sophie incredulously. Then she stammered, "Oh, my dear! I'm so sorry. I thought that's what was bothering you." Miss Anne placed a hand over her heart, as if she were taking a vow to tell the truth.

"What about Miss Ruth?" Sophie asked, leaning forward in her chair a little. Miss Anne let out a quick little breath and closed her eyes in embarrassment.

"What about Miss Ruth?" Sophie repeated, and when Miss Anne opened her eyes, she saw in Sophie's face a complete and absolute insistence on an answer, yet something of some concern for this woman who had been like an older sister to her for all those years.

"You know how she is," Miss Anne prefaced the statement that she knew would be so painful for Sophie to hear. "And I just assumed you'd heard what she's been saying about you and . . ." Miss Anne's voice trailed off, and she patted her chest as if in contrition.

Mea culpa!

"About me and . . . what?"

"It's *who,* not what. About you and Mr. Oto." There. It was said, this terrible gossip that she, herself, was now a party to spreading. And to the one it would hurt the most. "I'm so sorry," Miss Anne added, reaching over to put her hand over Sophie's. "I thought you knew. I thought it was why you seemed to be upset."

"What . . . what *about* me and Mr. Oto?" Sophie breathed.

"Well, how you painted together at the river on Sunday mornings, that's all."

So, Sophie was thinking, *someone saw us, after all. But why not? We never tried to hide anything.*

"Of course," Miss Anne went on, "I know there was nothing to it, but Ruth just . . . just makes too much of everything."

"She's a dirty old biddy!" Sophie said, her face flaming and her eyes flashing an anger Miss Anne had never seen in them before.

"I'm so sorry," Miss Anne said again. "I thought you knew."

Sophie took a deep breath and then looked at Miss Anne as if she had suddenly remembered that she was sitting there. Miss Anne's own face was a deep red, and her expression was so distressed that Sophie's anger was immediately replaced by a deep concern for the feelings of her old friend.

"It's not your fault, Miss Anne. I guess I'd rather have heard it from you than from anyone else." They sat in silence for a few moments before Sophie went on. "Mr. Oto and I did paint together, but it was purely innocent. There was nothing more to it than that."

Even as Sophie uttered the words, she knew that they were true. And, at the same time, that they were not true. True, in that they had painted together and also true, that it was innocent. But not true that there was nothing more to it. Not, at least, for her. She knew that because of the withered sprig of bougainvillea still on her dresser.

"Just what does Miss Ruth think we were doing?" Sophie asked finally, because she may as well know the whole terrible story, now that she knew this much.

"Oh, nothing, dear. You know how she is."

"All too well," Sophie admitted.

"And besides," Miss Anne continued. "It's the attack on Pearl Harbor, too. It changed us all." *Lordy!* she was thinking. *It certainly did that!* "But Mr. Oto's gone now. So it's all in the past. She'll forget about it soon. Get started thinking of something else, and then it will all be over."

Yes, Sophie was thinking. *She'll forget about it soon. Because nothing lasts.*

· 141 ·

Later Miss Anne brewed a pot of tea for the two of them, and they drank it sitting at the kitchen table, sitting close together, too, as if they were huddling against a cold neither of them could understand.

Chapter Twenty-one

Miss Anne said:

I felt so bad for Sophie that day, and I came close to telling her about Mr. Oto, just so she would know it wasn't Ruth's gossiping that made him go away. But then I thought maybe that would worry Sophie even more, knowing that Mr. Oto was still around. And of course, she would wonder why I'd lied about him, and then I would have to tell her everything. So I didn't say anything. Not right then, I didn't.

But sometimes, fate has a way of pushing us right to the brink, and that's what happened on Friday morning when—purely and simply—I lost my footing going down the back steps and fell and broke my ankle. And of course, word about it got around real fast, and I wound up with a lot more help than I really wanted.

All the ladies formed up a veritable parade and marched in and out, bearing platters of cold fried chicken and bowls of potato salad. And of course,

Eulalie was at the head of the pack, bawling orders like a lead hound—even though she'd just gotten back in town from visiting her sister in Savannah only a few hours before.

After the good doctor came and put a cast on my ankle, and admonished me to stay off my feet for at least a month, the first thing he said was that he should find a woman to come and take care of me. Because I would need more help than what Mr. Oto could do for me. And that's when I told him that Mr. Oto was gone. Surprised me a bit, that did—him not knowing Mr. Oto was gone, what with Ruth's tendency to spread news all over town and with Eulalie's big ears for gossip.

I didn't say anything like that, of course, but he knew that's what I was thinking, so he volunteered as to how Eulalie had been away visiting her sister in Savannah and was coming back the next morning. And that's why he hadn't heard any of the news, of course.

So without even asking me, he took it upon himself to get Big Sally to come and stay with me. Now, if I'd known that's who was coming, I'd have had a fit about it. Because everyone in town knew about Big Sally. Lived in a little house down by the bridge and supported herself by doing day work at one time or another for just about all the ladies in town. But she was such a stickler for things being clean, most folks spent two or three days cleaning up before she came, just so they wouldn't feel so embarrassed. Didn't do a bit of good, though, because Big Sally just stomped around and snorted something terrible, just as if she had *never* seen such filth—before she started in to scrubbing and cleaning with a vengeance and grumbling about it the whole time.

"Scrubbed the pattern right off my kitchen linoleum!" was one of the things I remembered hearing. "Made me feel like I'd been keeping a pigsty!"

And when Big Sally arrived, she was just as sullen as could be. Stomped right down the hallway, burst into my room, frowned at me—and said, "Gimme them sheets!" Why, she nearly tumbled me right out of the bed getting them out from under me. And the next morning, when folks started coming, bringing food and condolences for my misfortune, Big Sally answered the door every single time as if it were a deliberate affront to her attempts to get my house good and clean. A couple of the ladies even whispered to me that they thought for sure she would make them take off their shoes—*for goodness' sake!*—before she'd let them come inside.

As I said, Eulalie was first, and she showed up before nine o'clock, carrying a coconut cake that was still warm from the oven, a platter of freshly fried chicken, and a big basket of biscuits. She hadn't even changed her traveling clothes, but had gone into her kitchen and started cooking for me, just as soon as she heard about my ankle, when the doctor met her bus.

Right behind her came Ruth and fully half the membership of the local DAR chapter, and they all ignored Big Sally completely, even carrying all the dining room chairs into my room and perching all around and staying for a long time, "to keep me company." But toward the end of their visit, I began wondering when Sophie was going to come. Because as soon as I realized I had hurt myself, the only thing that was on my mind was that someone was going to have to take over with the supply line to Mr. Oto, and Sophie was the only one I knew of that I could trust completely. But I didn't think she would come as long as Ruth was there.

Finally, all those good ladies were ready to depart, and they carefully stacked all their plates and cups on my dresser—because they were afraid to take them back into the kitchen. So I was the one who had to listen to Big Sally's muttering and snarling when she came in with more clean sheets for my bed and saw the dishes there. But I had other things to think about.

The very next night, Mr. Oto would be expecting me to show up like I was supposed to and leave some fresh clothes and some canned goods by the big palm tree. And especially, fresh water. What would he think when I didn't come? Worse, perhaps he would try and sneak back into town, come to my house and see what was wrong with me. Certainly, he'd come at night, but suppose someone saw him? Then everyone would know that I had tried to hide him. Maybe I would even be sent to prison. For treason!

It was a terrible time for me, lying there alone with it and wondering where Sophie was. Big Sally clattered dishes and scrubbed the very life out of my kitchen linoleum and stripped my bed again, even though it didn't need stripping. Eulalie stopped by once more, bringing enough food to feed a hundred people. And still Sophie didn't come.

Toward dusk, I made up my mind that I would simply have to send Big Sally over to Sophie's house with a note—if she would take it, that is. Because there wasn't anything else I could do. I couldn't get to the phone in the hallway and I couldn't ask Big Sally to call for me, because it was common knowledge around town that she wouldn't use a telephone at all. Someone once told her that if a storm came up while she was using it, she would get electrocuted by the lightning.

But thank goodness, just about the time when I was getting myself worked up into a real lather about it, Sophie came. And I was never so glad to see anyone in my whole life. Strange thing, too, that Big Sally never grumbled at all when Sophie came. Even escorted her to the door of my room and said, "Miss Sophie is here to see you." And she had a right pleasant tone in her voice, too. But I didn't have time to think for long about such things. Because the very minute I laid eyes on Sophie, I made a sudden and vital decision about something I'd been turning over in my mind—whether to tell her *everything*. I mean, about Mr. Oto being from a Japanese family. Because I'd been banking on her thinking that even someone who was Chinese— and not Japanese at all—would still be worried enough about being mistaken for one that he would hide away somewhere. But it was only fair to tell her. Because if I was going to ask her to get involved, she certainly deserved to know the whole story. And maybe even to think about what would happen to us all, if we got caught.

But even with all that going through my mind, I was so glad to see her that my eyes filled up the minute she walked into the room. She was wearing her mama's black coat—one that I recognized from years ago, and it was too big for Sophie, so that it rested upon her shoulders more like a cape.

"Are you okay, Miss Anne?" she asked me, coming forward toward the bed and acting like she was going to bend down and kiss me, except that she thought better of it and kind of stopped in a little half-bow—reminded me so much of Mr. Oto that I reached and took hold of the sleeve of her coat and pulled her close so that I could whisper to her. I certainly didn't want Big Sally to hear what I had to tell Sophie.

"I'm so glad you've come, Sophie," I said, most honestly. "Please listen. I need you to do something very important for me and not tell a soul," I whispered to her, and she looked at me in a worried way, as if she were wondering if I were in my right mind. Especially after all that time of her putting up with her crazy Aunt Minnie, you see. So that was something else I had to worry about— that even after I told her about Mr. Oto, she would think I was senile and didn't know what I was talking about.

But she said, "What is it, Miss Anne?" Now she was leaning close to me again and so I released her sleeve.

"You have to take some supplies to Mr. Oto, where he's hiding out in my papa's old fishing cabin." There. It was said. The terrible secret.

And I wish you could have seen her face. I'd thought quite a bit about how she might react. Maybe be real shocked or confused and ask me a lot of questions, the most likely one being about why I had lied. But she didn't.

Still, something or other flickered across her eyes, and it certainly wasn't any worried look or shock or confusion at all. Why, she almost brightened, and if I hadn't known better, I'd have sworn on a stack of Bibles that she was working very hard to keep herself from smiling. That's when I thought just for a minute that maybe Ruth was right. Maybe there had been something going on. More than just painting. But what? After all, Sophie was a real lady. I knew that much.

Sophie certainly did start asking me questions then, but they were all about how she could find the cabin. I tried to explain to her that she had only to leave supplies by the palm tree, but she was real emphatic about the cabin itself, and she repeated back to me every single bit of the directions I gave to her. I kept trying to get to the part about Mr. Oto being from a Japanese family, but she kept interrupting me to ask more questions about how to get to the cabin.

Then, she was in such a hurry; I think she would have turned around and dashed right off, without thinking— if I hadn't reminded her not to let Sally see her leave in such a hurry. Reluctantly, she took off her coat and sat down, but she pulled her chair close to the bed so that we could speak privately, in low voices.

And still, I couldn't find a way to say what needed saying. I had the impression that she wasn't listening to much of anything right then. Just wanted to go ahead and take the supplies to Mr. Oto. I almost thought that she didn't realize how I had lied about him, much less why. But there were too many arrangements for us to make for me to figure anything out right then and there. I'd just have to take it a bit at a time.

"Just fresh water this time," I whispered. "Because he's got plenty of canned goods to last him until we get things all figured out."

"What things?"

Clearly, she was still anxious to leave, but I knew— even if she didn't—that we had to be very careful and plan everything out. Maybe it all had to do with the questions she wasn't asking.

"How to get this done without anyone knowing," I said, quite carefully.

"Oh."

It was a small and almost deflated utterance. Plainly, she simply hadn't had time to think everything through. Yet. And I was thinking that surely, she would have plenty of questions for me later. And later was the right time for handling them.

But all in all, I felt so much better about it. Especially because she *hadn't* acted shocked about finding out that Mr. Oto wasn't in Canada after all. And now, we were in it together, Sophie and me, no matter where it led us.

Chapter Twenty-two

*I*t was close to dusk when Sophie left Miss Anne's house, and she had to make a concerted effort to walk with reasonable slowness, so that she seemed merely to be strolling home from visiting with Miss Anne. But under the coat—her mama's coat—her heart was pumping so warm and strong that it almost drove her feet to dance all by themselves, and a delirious song to burst from her lips.

He isn't gone, after all. He's here, and tonight I'll see him again.

It was harder and harder for her to walk slowly, for what she really wanted to do was to skip and sing at the top of her lungs all the way down the middle of the street, like she'd done once as a child.

And Sophie was so deeply intent upon keeping her feet on the ground that when she passed Miss Ruth's house, she failed to notice Miss Ruth herself in the deep shadow of the front porch, where she had paused in watering her begonias to watch Sophie pass.

Well, I'm sure glad Sophie's sweet mama passed on before she could suffer the humiliation of a thankless child like that. One who's been keeping company with a gardener, for Heaven's sake—and a foreigner to boot!—and almost dark enough to be colored, sure enough! And an infidel! Miss Ruth thought.

Sophie, of course, had no idea that Miss Ruth was watching her, and as it happened, it was—unfortunately—right in front of Miss Ruth's house that Sophie's steps slowed and almost stopped—not for any effort on Sophie's part, but of their own volition.

My Lord! Sophie was thinking. *Miss Anne knows he's Japanese! That's why she lied about him!*

That terrible thought dragged at her heels so hard that momentarily she stopped altogether. Then she moved ahead, but at a very slow and pensive pace.

Miss Ruth, who was still watching, wondered to herself, *Well, what on earth was that all about?*

When Sophie left her house very late that same night, she wore her rain slicker, even though the night was very clear and calm. Because she was carrying bottles of water in both deep pockets, the slicker rested heavily upon her shoulders as she went through the quiet street of the sleeping town and on out along the sandy road beyond.

In her darkened bedroom, Miss Ruth was lying awake, as she often did of late. The deep, sweet sleep of health and relative youth had disappeared long ago for her. Sleep was something she had to dive down into. Work hard at it. As if she were wearing some kind of waterwings that kept her buoyed up toward wakefulness, no matter what careful bedtime ritual she practiced—the hot chocolate and the quiet reading. Nothing helped.

So she tossed and turned until she was irritable and afraid. What was it about the dark that bothered her so much? And wasn't there a poem about raging against the dying of the light? Maybe that was it.

Grumbling, she threw back the covers and walked over to the window—sometimes, looking out at the palm trees standing quietly in the darkness and at the empty street, she could picture that scene in full daylight. And it helped.

But it wasn't the usual imaginary daylight Miss Ruth saw through her window that night. It was Sophie—wearing a rain slicker and hurrying down the edge of the street before bolting across it and disappearing out toward the marsh.

What on earth is she *up to? Running around at all hours?* Miss Ruth smiled, and suddenly, she didn't mind at all that she was not able to fall asleep.

Sophie was nearly at the big palm when the moon arose over the treetops, and she didn't need a flashlight anymore to lead her to where Miss Anne had told her to leave the bottles of water for Mr. Oto to find. But when she reached the tree at last, she noticed the narrow path through the palmettos, and without a moment of hesitation, she followed it, knowing that at the very end of it, he would be waiting.

In the dark cabin, Mr. Oto slept, dreaming that he was tending the flowers in his father's garden with the warm California sun glowing against his back. His grandmother was standing in front of where he was working in the flower beds, and he could see her feet encased in tiny, brocaded shoes, and he heard her saying, ". . . so that the great crane turned into a beautiful bride who came to the old woodcutter's hut to bring him love and good fortune."

Then, in the dream, he stood and looked past her tiny shoulders to the snow-covered land where the great cranes were dancing with their wings spread wide and their heads pointed toward the heavens. The great, horned feet prancing and dancing in the pure snow and the red streaks on their heads against the white snow and the white feathers like silent fireworks.

One lone crane, a female with no mate, separated herself from the dancing flock and walked toward him slowly. Majestic head held high. And the deep eyes gazing at him out of the glare of winter sun.

But even in his sleep, Mr. Oto knew of the movement of the blanket nailed over the open doorway, and he sat up, half-asleep and looking at where the Crane-Wife stood, gazing down at him and with the beam of a bright light coming from her eyes to illuminate the darkness.

Chapter Twenty-three

When Sophie pushed aside the blanket from the open doorway of the cabin and shone the flashlight inside, she was completely startled by Mr. Oto's face directly in its beam, even though she knew he would be there. But nothing could have prepared her for this face.

Certainly, this was the same kind and gentle face, but now wreathed in a glow of childlike wonder. If ever she had doubted him, that doubt dissipated now. This was, most assuredly, not the face of an enemy. Not in any way.

She stood silently in the confirmed gladness, looking at the way his hand reached toward her, a gesture that at one time both broke her heart and gladdened it.

Such a gesture she had seen only once before, when her Aunt Minnie had called to her in the middle of one night and Sophie had gone to her room, anticipating that she would be disoriented and confused, as she usually was. But that hadn't happened. Instead, Aunt Minnie was in one of her last lucid states that Sophie could remember, and she held out her hand to Sophie in just such a way. And Sophie had sat on the side of her bed while they talked and laughed together for hours.

"I know what you've been doing," Aunt Minnie laughed, looking sideways, the way she always did when she was teasing, instead of that full-face stare with nothing behind her eye.

"What have I been doing?"

"It's the birds," she answered. "In the pantry."

"What about them?"

"You didn't throw them out like I told you to do."

"I wanted to."

"But you didn't."

"No."

"You put them all in a box, though."

"Yes ma'am. I did that."

"Why didn't you throw them out?"

"Because they were Mama's."

"They weren't your mama's," she said emphatically. "Birds don't belong to anyone except to themselves; throw them out. Find something that will last."

"You have come." His voice was so soft that she barely heard it, almost as if the words were those he was afraid to speak.

"Yes, I have come," she answered, moving into the room and carefully replacing the blanket back over the doorway while he lit the kerosene lantern and its comforting light filled the inside of the cabin.

"Did you see it?" he asked.

But she didn't even hear the question, for her eyes had fallen upon the painting of the Crane-Wife. And she was face-to-face with the pale, slender arms and the smooth, unlined face. Herself. So that was the mysterious painting he did not think was worthy for her to see! And was that beautiful lady in it truly her? Is that the way he saw her? Like that? It was almost more than she could comprehend.

Very slowly it became obvious to her—and with no doubt whatsoever—that this painting had been created by an artist who deeply loved his subject. Undeniable truth.

Love portrayed, too, in the powerful, sensual image of the huge bird behind her in the painting, its wings spread out in imitation of her own arms, and each wispy feather captured in paint against the deeper green of the shadows and the palmettos near the live oak tree.

"Did you see it?" he repeated.

"The painting?" Sophie whispered, still gazing at it, taking into her own being everything that was in the heart of the artist. *How could I not have known?* she wondered.

"No, not the painting," he replied. "The great crane itself. It's right outside. I saw it only a little while ago."

Sophie waited before answering. "Nothing is outside," she finally said, but she didn't know what her words were.

"Well, it's gone again, then," Mr. Oto said. Then he added, "But you are here."

Sophie tried to look at him, but her eyes refused to move from the painting. "It's very, very beautiful," she whispered finally.

"You don't mind?" The question was a very old one, worn smooth around the edges from having been in his thoughts for so long.

"I don't mind," she whispered. Then, "What is the bird?"

"The great crane. From outside, tonight. But earlier, from Miss Anne's own garden," he said. "And before that, from the land of my father's ancestors. And a very old story about happiness." He did not add *and love*. Because he didn't have to. She knew. He could tell—she *knew*.

For long minutes, neither of them said anything else. Sophie gazed at the painting until she had imprinted its every element into her being forever. In complete silence he waited, until at last, she turned her eyes upon his. And for the first time, she could identify what was in their depths—and it was the most incredible thing, something she hardly knew how to recognize. But recognize it, she certainly did.

Remembering then all the way back to her childhood, where she sat on the foot of Miss Anne's bed, watching her making tatted edges for the pillowcases in her hope chest, and asking, "How do you know if he loves you?"

"Oh, I know," Miss Anne had answered.

"But how?" Sophie had persisted.

"I can see it in his eyes."

But until that day so many years later and in the old fishing cabin, Sophie had not understood. Now, she was looking right at it—the incredible thing she could never have described to anyone, or understood from what anyone else said about it.

"Have I offended you?" His voice came through the fog of memory.

"Oh, no. You haven't offended me in the least," Sophie said. "But you have surprised me."

"I know," he answered. "I would rather that you had not seen it."

"Why?"

Sophie's question was genuine. And more than just a question about the painting itself.

"I think perhaps it tells too much—about what I have no right to feel."

To this, Sophie did not answer. For she was watching the new feeling deep inside her, also something that, perhaps, she had no right to feel, either.

"How is it you have come here?" he asked, seeing that she had curled inward, toward her own being, and also knowing that it had been enough, what was said between them. For now, at least. "How did you know where I was?" he asked.

"Miss Anne told me. She hurt her ankle and has to stay off it for a while, but it's nothing serious. And she trusted me with the secret. I'm so glad she did."

"It is a trust well placed," he said. "What she—and now *you* have done for me is probably a very dangerous thing."

"Yes, I understand that now," Sophie answered. "I've read the papers and listened to the radio. I know all about the rage people are feeling and about the fear everyone has of the . . . of your people."

"I assure you as I did Miss Anne," he said carefully. "I am an American."

"I know." Sophie smiled at him, feeling yet another surge of relief. Not the enemy. Not this man. Not this man who loved her.

Somehow, it was all becoming more than she could think about, so that she felt as if she were dividing into two—like an amoeba—one cell of her wanting nothing more than to be with him forever, the other crying for solitude so that she could taste this most delicious reality. Every wonderful drop of it. Feel every feeling. Taste every joy.

"Here, this is for you." She remembered the outward purpose of her trip to the cabin and drew forth the bottles of fresh water, holding them out to him. "Miss Anne said you would need these right away. And when I come again, I'll bring more."

He took the bottles from her as if he were receiving a great gift, and his hands touched hers and did not draw away. For a long moment, he held her by the barest touch of his hands and with his great, dark eyes.

Chapter Twenty-four

Miss Anne said:

Sophie came back to see me the first chance she had the very next day, as I knew she would do, to let me know if she had found the big palm. But of course, she had to wait until Ruth and all her whole entourage had made their daily call, with Big Sally stomping around, being just as unpleasant as she dared to be and enjoying every minute of it.

And the whole time, I was thinking that Ruth was looking at me in a very strange way. But she never said a thing, except for the usual chitchat. And of course, I was all caught up in thinking of Mr. Oto and wondering if Sophie had found the big palm after all.

Finally, finally, the ladies all left—with Ruth casting one more of her strange glances at me—and then I began waiting for Sophie to come. It would have been so much easier if I could have used the phone, but of course, it was all the way down the hall.

Once again, I knew for a fact when it was Sophie knocking at my door because Big Sally was really quite pleasant to her—and even pleasant to me, too, the whole time Sophie was there with me.

"He's fine." Sophie smiled around the words, after she closed the bedroom door and pulled the chair up close to my bed. Once again, I noticed how pretty she looked. But no time for thinking about that.

"You saw him?" I asked, somewhat surprised and wondering how on earth she could find the old cabin what with only those few directions I had given to her.

"I saw him," she answered, and she looked me right in the eyes and never wavered her gaze in the least little bit.

"And he's okay?" I asked, because her steady gaze made me feel somewhat uncomfortable, and I had to say *something*.

"He's fine . . . except . . . well, he says he's seen some kind of crane, and I'm not sure he really has."

"Well, I expect he has, what with his being right there by the river."

"Not like the cranes around here," Sophie said. "This one is very large, with great wings and a bright red crest."

"No, I've never heard of one like that," I admitted. "Have you seen it?"

"I've seen a painting he did of it," Sophie said, and for some reason, her cheeks reddened. "I didn't see the crane myself, but he told me he first saw it in your own garden."

I was thinking then. About the time when Mr. Oto told me the story of the crane who became a bride for the old woodcutter. And told me how he *thought* he saw such a crane in my garden.

"He said he thought he saw something like that one time," I said. "But I didn't see it."

"Perhaps he's only imagining it," Sophie suggested—rather reluctantly, I thought.

"Perhaps." After all, Mr. Oto himself had said there was just such a possibility. But there was something else I had on my mind by then, for I still had not told her what needed to be said.

"You haven't asked me anything about Mr. Oto. Not really," I said, finally.

"I don't need to." Sophie answered back so quickly that I knew she'd already turned over all the possibilities in her mind.

"So you do know how important it is that no one sees you go there?"

"I understand," she said.

Still, I was worried about it. Just seemed to me as if Sophie wasn't thinking all that clearly. But I decided I needn't worry about it—not right away, at least—for, after all, she wouldn't be going again until the next Sunday night.

So that was all we said about it. We both knew everything there was to know. And I still, to this day, think it was awfully good of Sophie to go all that way and even find the cabin itself. To make sure that Mr. Oto was all right. And I certainly felt better, after that, knowing that someone was looking out for him. I just wanted her to be careful. And I'd certainly remind her of that—before the next Sunday.

Chapter Twenty-five

$\mathscr{B}$ut just as Sophie had asked no questions of Miss Anne, likewise, Miss Anne had asked no questions of Sophie either, for which Sophie was grateful. Because she had not left the cabin until very late—or very early, depending upon how you thought of it. In fact, as she hurried back into town, the first pale shades of dawn were barely visible in the night sky. And how would that look if anyone saw her? Especially snoopy old ladies like Miss Ruth? Old ladies who always want to think the worst. Think there was something dirty about it.

They would never believe that Sophie and Mr. Oto had spent the long, lovely night just sitting close together in the soft glow of the kerosene lantern, sometimes talking, but more often simply listening together to the sounds of the night creatures and then the barely perceptible gurgle of the river as the tide changed in the ocean. The high tide sent a ripple of water back up the river to swirl against the mangrove roots and slap against the eroded banks. Almost music, the rhythmic sounds of the night.

To all this, they had listened together, with the portrait gazing at them. And they had held each other's hands until the lamp burned low and Sophie knew that the morning would soon come.

Somehow, without her stirring or saying a word, he knew that she must go. And it was then that he spoke. "Will you come again? Tonight?" he asked.

"Yes," she answered simply. And it made everything right. When she hurried back along the road in the early, early light, it was the only thing on her mind.

After Sophie left Miss Anne's house, she went home, and even though she expected to feel quite sleepy, there was some kind of an exhilarated energy in her, so that she could not rest. Instead, she fried a chicken to golden tenderness and baked a pan full of biscuits. By the time she had finished, washed and dried all the dishes, and wrapped the chicken carefully in waxed paper and put it in the refrigerator, her cheeks were a bright pink from the heat of the kitchen.

Strange, she thought. *For the weather to have turned so warm.*

Later, she went into her bedroom, pulled the shades down against the early afternoon sun, turned back the bedspread, and stretched out with only the cool sheet covering her. She didn't expect to fall asleep, but she did. Almost instantly.

And the dream was waiting for her—came upon her

with a force that exhilarated her and left her strangely unafraid. A dream so real that she could feel the wind full on her face, lifting her hair. A swirling and fickle wind that first pushed and then pulled her so that her feet in the silent sand moved in a mindless dance that pulled her only slowly toward the edge of the underbrush where she saw the minuscule crease of sand between the palmettos. Drunkenly, she approached it, both fearing and loving the darkness. And once inside the thicket, she felt her face glowing in the sudden stillness.

At first, she only sensed the presence of the great crane. Breathed in the musty, warm aroma of its healthy feathers. When he finally stepped forth in the full majesty and fragile beauty of all nature, he was so wonderful a creature that she could hardly breathe.

He fixed her with his great dark eyes and then slowly drew himself to his full height, the eyes beginning to glow a deep and soft violet in the darkness. The great wings lifted out bit by bit, and he came toward her, still holding her with his eyes. Finally, he was so close that she could reach out to touch the snowy breast, to feel the strong, warm feathers and look into the eyes that shone a deep and glowing purple.

Wings that came forward, deep pinions and shoulder blades of the wing bones embracing, and the eyes willing her—until *impossibly!*—her shoulders, still tenderly cradled by the great wings, touched the warm sand. The crane bending over her in an arc of love.

She awakened slowly, to the lovely ache deep within

her and the warm film of perspiration on her skin like a veil. Surprised that the room was so warm—*how strange, in mid-December!*—she threw back the sheet, and the aroma that filled the room was the perfume of her own awakened body.

It was almost midnight when Sophie slipped out of the house, once again wearing the rain slicker, but this time with one pocket laden with paper-wrapped cold fried chicken and the other with biscuits. The air was surprisingly still—muggy and oppressive as she hurried along the silent street, and farther along, under the great trees along the sandy lane at the other end of town, she noticed how very still the night air was, with the Spanish moss hanging in limp hanks. And such a silence over everything, so that not a creature even scurried in the underbrush as she hurried past.

Miss Ruth was sitting in her dark bedroom and watching through the window. This time, waiting. Distinctly waiting. She had nearly dozed off a few times, but pulled herself back to wakefulness by the enticement of the living room lights still burning and also Sophie's bedroom light. And Sophie's shadow moving across the bedroom from time to time. So Miss Ruth knew that something was going on.

It was nearly midnight when the lights went out, first in the bedroom and then in the living room, and Sophie came down the front steps. Once again, she was wearing the slicker, and she darted across the quiet street and toward the far end of town.

What are you up to, Sophie? Miss Ruth wondered. *If I were younger I'd go right out behind you and follow you to wherever you're going, because you're up to no good, and I owe it to your mama, at least, to find out what's going on and where it is you're running off to every night. Like a harlot!*

Chapter Twenty-six

*I*n the cabin, Sophie and Mr. Oto sat together on a cloth spread upon the floor, with the paper packets of chicken and biscuits between them and the kerosene lamp lending even more warmth to the humid air. Once again, under the gaze of the great crane in the painting, they sat together, saying little, but looking at each other frequently and smiling in deep contentment.

Mr. Oto thought that Sophie looked especially beautiful on that night, and sensed something new in her spirit, so that she smiled more often and laughed aloud—a soft, pleased laugh—when he said that the fried chicken was very good. Very good, indeed.

At last, he wiped his hands carefully and then stood up, holding a hand down to Sophie. "Come with me," he said in such a soft voice that, at first, Sophie did not know she heard him.

"Where?" And just as soon as she had asked, she realized that it didn't matter.

"Just come with me, please. I want to show you something."

Sophie took his hand, somehow surprised at its warmth and softness, and after she stood, he did not release it, but blew out the lantern and led her to the doorway. *Is he going to take me with him to try and find that strange crane?* she wondered. *And what if he sees it and I don't? Like Miss Anne?*

She followed him through the darkness, in and among the trees and with the sounds of the river beside them, until they crossed a small wooden bridge Sophie had not known was there and then came into the edge of sand dunes. A gentle whispering just beyond the dunes, and when they finally crested the last one, the ocean lay before them, in the dark, with the river's mouth open to its gentle swells.

Mr. Oto leaned back and looked straight up into the dome of stars above them.

"There is your sky," he said simply. And Sophie looked also.

Yes, she thought, *There is my sky.*

High above them, the endless heavens, the multitude of stars, some of them so far away that they could only guess their glitterings, and here they stood on the sandy bottom of eternity, and at the last, it was only his firm hand that kept her from soaring like an everlasting meteor into the heavens.

Then the same warm and gentle hand leading her past the dunes and out onto the flat, dark beach. He released her then and, stooping, removed his shoes and rolled up his trouser legs. Likewise, she removed her shoes and they walked forward and into the ocean until the tepid and slow-moving water was caressing their knees.

"The sea is too calm tonight," Mr. Oto said.

"And so warm," Sophie added. "It must be the Gulf Stream. But that doesn't usually come this time of year."

"You know much about this ocean," he said. "As I know about the Pacific near my father's house in California."

Sophie didn't answer him, because whatever was in the words, they called for no response whatsoever from her. In fact, she thought that he sounded as if he were speaking only to himself. And before she could even wonder at that, she knew—without any doubt—why he had brought her to where the river and the ocean melted into each other.

"You're going away." She heard her own voice stating what she knew to be true. But how she knew, she couldn't guess.

"Yes. I must. For Miss Anne's sake. And for yours. You must not endanger yourselves for me any longer. Miss Anne was right. The people are enraged, and there is great danger. So I will go very quietly, and no one will know this has ever been."

I will know, Sophie wanted to say. "And will you come back?" she said instead.

He didn't answer right away. Around them, the ocean swells had begun to grow very gradually, and a strange, too-warm breeze moved across the face of the black water.

"When the madness of this war is over, I will come back. If you *want* me to come back." And he was thinking to himself, *If there were any way, my dear Sophie, I would take you with me. But there is no place for us. For surely, as my wife, you, too, would have become the enemy!*

"Yes," she said. "I want that very much." And she didn't say: *And until that day, I will come to this place often, to look into the endless sky and to know that you are also beneath the same stars. And that will be enough.*

The large and very sudden swell came from behind her, lifting her slightly so that her feet were as light as feathers upon the wet sand below, while at the same instant, she saw his eyes widen and his hands come up to catch her. The swell pressing against her from behind, thrusting her solidly against him. He stood as immovable as a tree, his hands gripping her shoulders, steadying her as the swell receded. But the ocean did not pull her back as it had thrust her forward. It left her solidly against him and with the warm skin of him under her surprised palms.

In his black eyes—those deep, kind eyes—she saw the twin reflections of her own face. Reflections that came closer and closer until she could no longer tell which was her face and which was his. Then the gentle shock of his warm mouth and the surprising strength of his arms sliding around her shoulders and encompassing her. The incredible oneness with the earth. With the sea and with the sand. And even with the multitude of stars high above. The tempo of the universe in her own jugular vein and the melting of all the edges of everything that separated her from the night. And from him.

Then, finally, his stepping backward and the deep sigh of incredulity that escaped them both.

"Are you all right?" he finally managed to whisper, and for one confusing moment, she thought he was referring to what had just passed between them.

But he meant the wave. Of course.

They walked back to the cabin in silence and with the stars hanging down around them so closely that they could almost reach up and touch them. And even if they had noticed the low, scudding clouds that were coming up and over the black horizon above the black ocean, they would not have cared.

Near dawn, Sophie walked back home, and it was a disturbing walk, indeed. With her thinking that at any moment the great crane of her dream would step out of the darkness before her, with its eyes glowing and its beautiful, white wings outspread. And if that happened, she would turn, most assuredly, and go straight back to the cabin. To him. Tell him that she would go with him, no matter where he went and no matter what happened to them.

But the crane didn't appear.

Chapter Twenty-seven

At midmorning the next day, Miss Ruth went out into her front yard, pretending to pluck dead and discolored leaves from her dwarf azaleas, but really looking to see if Sophie's bedroom shades were up yet.

They weren't.

Miss Ruth peered at her wristwatch. *Ten-fifteen, and she's not up yet. What time did she come home? And where did she go, so late in the night?*

So that Miss Ruth plucked only a few more leaves before she went back inside her house, put on a light sweater against the rising wind, and walked off down the street, depending only upon her sharp sense of right and wrong to provide vital clues into what she was convinced were Sophie's transgressions.

She walked along slowly, swinging her arms a little and perhaps even convincing herself that she was merely out for a nice walk on a beautiful morning. But the resolve of her purpose was ever with her, for after all, she'd known Sophie's mother nearly her whole life, since they were both quite young—and she'd known Sophie ever since the day she was born. So it was her *responsibility* to try to find out what was going on. In memory of her old friend, and for the sake of that friend's wayward daughter.

Just like her father, she is. And Willis had come calling on me first—until he changed his mind. So Sophie should have been my daughter. And I'll certainly do right by her, no matter what it takes.

On toward the end of town she went, passing the last houses and strolling on down the unpaved road toward the marsh, and with the midmorning sun glowing and yet with a strange stillness in the air. Especially strange for that time of year. Almost as if the world were holding its breath in anticipation of what she would find out.

She moved ever forward, not knowing what she was looking for, but determined to find something—anything—that would solve the mystery of Sophie's nocturnal wanderings. For Miss Ruth knew, without any doubt whatsoever, that Sophie had been going somewhere definite and distinct. Because of the resolve in her steps. That was for sure. It wasn't just a nighttime stroll though that would have been suspicious, right by itself.

No, Miss Ruth thought as she took off the light sweater. *She was going somewhere. Somewhere specific. Only where?*

In the cabin, Mr. Oto slept only fitfully. The long, wonderful night with Sophie had left him saddened beyond his wildest dreams. How could it be that, at last, he had found his great love, but now all the insanity of war and the need for his running away and hiding like a thief was robbing him! And his resolve, in that half-sleep, was that he would come back for Sophie. He was sure of it.

Miss Ruth had moved far down the long road, and with the weather feeling so blustery and muggy, she was tempted to turn back. After all, she had come a long way already, and she still had to go all the way back. But something kept her going for just a little longer, and she decided she would walk only as far as that big palm tree she could see ahead, and if she couldn't find anything, she would turn around and go back.

She moved ever closer to the big tree, and beyond it, she could see only mile after mile of palmetto scrub, the road trailing off, straight and flat, into the distance. Finally, she reached the tree and stood, gratefully, in the shade of its fronds, while she caught her breath and rested for a few minutes before starting back to town. She had come a long way. Longer, even, than she had realized. Looking back down the road toward town, she anticipated the walk home, and with the sun rising ever higher and the weather turning even warmer than it had been. And now, no breeze at all, a strange thing in itself.

Finally, Miss Ruth shaded her eyes and looked back down the road toward town one more time before she would start back. But just as she started to turn from the big palm, she happened to look down and see tire tracks in the sand.

What on earth? Why would anyone pull over right here— out in the middle of nowhere?

And then, when she looked more closely, she saw not only tire tracks, but footprints, too, and leading to a crease in the palmetto bushes. It was then that Miss Ruth remembered the old fishing cabin that had belonged to Anne's father. Because once, when she and Anne were just little girls, Anne's papa had brought them to the cabin one afternoon, to show it to them. It was right after he had it built, and he was very proud of it.

Is that where you're going, Sophie? And if so—why?

And without another thought, Miss Ruth started off through the palmettos, following a trail that she had not walked since her childhood—remembering the deep sand beneath her feet and the lank, hanging moss in the trees, and, after a long walk, the cabin.

In the cabin, Mr. Oto still slept fitfully—unable, somehow, to fall into his usual deep and peaceful slumber. Something in the air, perhaps, he thought. Something very warm and almost oppressive—as if there were not a breath of air stirring. For the past hour or so, he had been concentrating on the chirping of tree frogs in the great live oaks, trying to gain some peace of mind. And rest.

But suddenly and without warning, the tree frogs fell utterly silent—all at once. A silence, in and of itself, that was almost deafening. And something else.

Someone was coming!

Sophie?

No, he thought at the last moment. Not Sophie. How he knew was a mystery to him, but so strong was his conviction that he slipped out of bed just as silently as a shadow, and across the room to lift the very edge of the torn blanket over the window.

Miss Ruth!

With her wizened and squinting face above the palmettos at the edge of the trees. And the bright sunlight flashing on her glasses. Lifting her hand and shading her eyes. Looking at the cabin.

Before Mr. Oto even had time to think, he stepped back across the room and rolled right under the cot, hardly daring to breathe and lying just as still as death, with his cheek against the rough planks of the cabin floor.

An oblique rectangle of sunlight across the floor when the torn blanket was pulled back, and he could see her feet. He hardly dared to breathe while the feet came forward and then turned slowly around in the center of the small room. And moved toward the box that was along the wall.

The painting!

The feet staying in that solitary place for a very long time, with the toes pointed at where the painting was propped up against the wall. His painting of Sophie as the Crane-Wife. And knowing that Miss Ruth was looking at it—with disdain, probably—violated everything he held dear.

· 178 ·

Sophie—*my dear Sophie!*—of course, whose lovely image was upon the paper, blessedly unaware of the ridicule to which it would certainly be subject in Miss Ruth's mind. And the great crane—that symbol of love and happiness!

And his father and the beauty of his gentle spirit. And the tale of magic and good fortune and fidelity that he had taken such pleasure in telling!

Lying in the dim light under the cot, Mr. Oto felt unfamiliar tears sliding down the side of his nose and dripping onto the floor.

And has it come to this? Hiding like an animal in a dark cave, while that despicable woman looks at everything I hold dear?

After what seemed like an eternity to Mr. Oto, the feet moved—toes pointing toward each wall and then moving, reluctantly it seemed, to the door and out of the cabin.

Chapter Twenty-eight

*M*iss Anne said:

It was early in the afternoon, I believe, when I started wondering if maybe Matilda had been right about a storm coming. Because the weather had turned quite warm and very still. So that my room felt musty and stale.

Big Sally came in, carrying an armful of freshly laundered sheets from the clothesline.

"Can't use these yet," she pronounced. "They're not dry all the way. Have to hang them inside." So saying, she temporarily dumped them on the foot of my bed and went to open my windows.

"Good," I said. "It's awfully warm in here."

"Outside, too," she grunted, shoving up the moisture-swollen windows. "Sheets should have dried by now. Been out there since morning. Too much water in the air for them. Too hot. Feel like satan sucking the breath right out of this old world," she said morosely, and then picked up the sheets and went back down the hallway.

And that's exactly the way it did feel.

Not too long after that, I was having the first good nap I'd had in a long time. Because I was feeling very much at peace for the first time since I'd come up with the idea of hiding Mr. Oto in the cabin. After all, Sophie was making sure Mr. Oto had food and water, and even though I was still worried about how she'd gone to the cabin itself, I knew that I didn't have to think about that again until before next Sunday— plenty of time for getting a hold of her and reminding her not to go to the cabin itself, but just to leave the supplies right where I'd told her to leave them in the first place.

So I was having quite a nice rest, when I heard hard knocking on the front door and Big Sally going down the hall to let them in—whoever it was—and her grumbling the whole way. I wondered who it could be, because most of my visitors made their calls during the morning hours, figuring quite rightly that I would spend most of the afternoon napping and recovering from my fall.

Only took me a minute to realize who it was coming to see me, because of hearing Ruth's little nervous tap-tapping steps coming down the long hallway toward my room.

Oh, Lord!

When Ruth came into my room, she had such a face on her—like I'd never seen before, and she plopped herself down in a chair without so much as a how-do-you-do and just sat there, staring at me.

"What's going on here?" she finally said, as if that made perfect sense.

"What do you mean?" I said, and I didn't try to hide the weariness in my voice, because I'd finally been able to relax, and I certainly didn't feel like playing any games with Ruth. Really I wanted just to tell her to take her old sourpuss face right on out of there and leave me alone. But of course, I didn't say anything like that.

"You know perfectly well what I mean," she shot back at me, and that really made me angry. How dare she come bursting into my room and acting so ugly—and with me in my sickbed?

"Listen, Ruth," I began, keeping my voice as calm as possible. "Whatever it is, just say it right out and let's dispense with all this cat-and-mouse conversation."

"Why, I *never* . . . ," she sputtered, and then she went right into her "Why, I'm just trying to help" defense, which she always did if someone called her hand. "I'm just a good Christian woman who thinks it's her duty to let you know." That's what she always said.

"Let me know what?" I asked, but something in the pit of my stomach was beginning to feel more than just a little alarmed, so I reached over to my bedside table for my fingernail file and started filing away at my nails, trying to look a little bored—or at the very least, completely unconcerned.

"That someone's using your papa's old fishing cabin, down by the river."

Well, there it was, then——the worst thing that could happen. But I still didn't know exactly what she had seen. Or who. Mr. Oto himself? Did she know already exactly who was using that old cabin?

"My papa's cabin?" I asked, stalling for time until I could figure out just how much she knew.

"*Your* papa's cabin. There's a kerosene lamp there and sheets on the cot. And the strangest picture——painting I've ever seen."

"Did you see who's there?" It was the question I had to ask, but inside, I could feel my heart cowering at what her answer might be.

"No." Has there ever been so sweet a word? "But it certainly has something to do with Sophie. I know that much."

"And just how do you know that?" I asked.

"Because the picture is of her. And some big egret or other. And besides, I've watched her going out of her house and down the street for two nights in a row. So this morning, I walked down that way . . . far on down the road, as you well know. And I found a little path through the palmettos. I thought I remembered your papa's cabin being down that way somewhere. And I followed that path right to it. It's a pretty well-used path, too."

I was thinking hard . . . thinking fast. Because everything hinged on whether or not I could throw Ruth off the track until we could make some other arrangements for hiding Mr. Oto. *Damn!*

"Sophie can go there if she wants to," I replied.

"So you knew about that, then!" I could sense an *Aha!* in her tone.

"I knew about it. Of course," I said.

"Well, I'll bet you didn't know that she's meeting somebody down there, did you?" Ruth sounded completely happy to drop that tidbit of gossip on me.

"That's ridiculous," I answered, but again in what I hoped sounded like a completely unconcerned tone of voice. "Sophie can use my papa's cabin anytime she wants to," I said.

"But what's she doing there?" Ruth wasn't going to let it alone. If I ever doubted that, I doubted it no longer.

"Painting, that's what," I said, warming to the idea of that explanation. For it certainly tied in quite nicely with what Ruth said about seeing a picture down there.

"Why would she need sheets on the bed for that?" Ruth shot back at me. And she wasn't through, yet. "You know, of course, that I never did believe that story you told about that foreign man of yours. I just wonder . . . are you hiding him out down there?"

And that's the precise moment when I realized that I was engaged in a very deadly exchange with her. Whatever faults Ruth may have had, and there were certainly plenty of them—just like with all of us—she wasn't stupid. So right then and there, I made up my mind what I had to do, even though I certainly didn't like doing it. Because in spite of Ruth's ugly gossip and the way it had already hurt Sophie, I still hated to do the same thing to her.

"Ruth, we've known each other for a long time, but I'm telling you to stop this gossiping about Sophie. And about some cock-and-bull story you've dreamed up about Mr. Oto. I want you to leave it alone."

"Leave what alone?" she asked, somewhat innocently. See? I told you she was plenty sharp.

"Whatever it is your dirty little mind is imagining," I said, and watched her face as those cruel words sank in. And I didn't enjoy it one little bit. Because Ruth and I were both raised to be as mannerly as possible—just like most Southern women, especially in little towns like this one—and this kind of open confrontation wasn't something either one of us was used to. Not really.

"Why, Anne!" She drew back in dismay, and I had to remind myself that this was her usual tack, whenever she suspected she was close to any kind of direct unpleasantness. I guess her philosophy was that it was all right to gossip like mad about someone, as long as you didn't hurt their feelings where you could see them suffering.

"I'm not through, Ruth," I said, and I lowered my voice a bit, just in case Big Sally was snooping around in the hallway outside my room. "You will stop this gossiping and stop it right now. Sophie is a fine, honorable lady. And Mr. Oto is gone. So you will not go to my papa's cabin again. But Sophie may go there anytime she pleases. Do you understand me?"

"No, as a matter of fact, I don't understand one little bit. What on earth has gotten into you, Anne?"

But I ignored her question. Because I'd gone too far by then to back down. Why, I'd looked her right in the face and flat-out, stomp-down lied. Not a light kind of lie, like Mr. Oto going to Canada. Because all I had to do, basically, was tell a few people and they spread it around for me. But this was a bald-faced, go-to-hell lie.

And you know, even all these years later, if I had it to do over again, I'd do it exactly the same way.

"Just you hear what I'm saying," I went on. Like I couldn't stop being mean, once I'd gotten started with it. "You leave Sophie alone. Or so help me, I'll . . . start spreading some gossip of my own."

"About what?" she asked smugly, and there it was again, that sanctimony. My own papa used to say: "God save me from the churchgoers who hang up their religion with their Sunday pants!" Mostly, he said that whenever Mama started in on him about his not going to church. "Talk better to God and listen better, too, right down there by the river," he used to say. And that's where he always spent his Sunday mornings. And a kinder, gentler, more honest and godly man never lived on this earth.

But I knew how Miss Ruth's papa used to go down to the cabin, too. And not for talking to God or for fishing, either. That was the ammunition I had to use now. To protect myself. And Mr. Oto. And Sophie.

"I'll tell everybody in town about how your own papa used to go down to that cabin, Ruth. And what for."

"What?" No good manners in her voice then, but a demand that indicated I'd better know what I was talking about. And I did.

"How he used to go down there every so often, and my own papa had to go along, just to take care of him. Keep him from falling into the river!"

Well, she certainly knew what I meant by that. Because Ruth's papa had been the bulwark of the Baptist Church. He was against laughing out loud on Sunday. Against dancing—anytime. Against strong drink, of course. But every once in a while, he'd go down to my papa's cabin and take a couple of bottles of fine Kentucky bourbon along with him and—tie one on.

I guess that was a rather vulgar way to put it, but it was true.

Ruth's face turned bloodred. Of course, she had known about that. But maybe she'd forgotten about it. Maybe having her head up in the air so high made her forget how things really were.

And you know, from the look on her face, I halfway expected her to have a massive stroke right then and there—fall across my bed just as dead as a doornail. But she didn't. She just stared and stared at me, like she couldn't believe what she was hearing.

"I mean it," I said, just to make sure she understood me completely.

She didn't say another thing, but reached down, picked up her pocketbook, and walked out in a huff. Left me lying there feeling like the meanest human being who ever lived—and also wondering, in another way, if what I'd done was wise or not. Because one of two things would happen—either she would leave it alone, believing that I certainly had meant what I said about spreading that mean gossip about her own papa, who'd been dead for thirty or forty years even then, or else my threat would convince her that there *was*, indeed, something going on at my papa's cabin. Maybe even that Mr. Oto was probably hiding there, sure enough.

And then she wouldn't stop until she found out everything there was to know.

My next thought was that I had to get hold of Sophie right away—warn her that Ruth knew she was going to the cabin. And also find out why on earth Sophie was going down there at all. For goodness' sake, she only had to take fresh water down there and leave it beside the big palm tree and that just on Sunday evenings. Nothing else was necessary. And maybe even get Sophie to find somewhere else we could hide Mr. Oto. Quickly.

"Sally?" I called, and while I listened to her heavy footsteps coming down the hall, I scrawled a quick, blunt note: "Come right away." And I folded it, sealed it in an envelope, and when Sally came into the room, I handed it to her. "Please take this down to Miss Sophie's house right away," I said. "It's very, very important."

Big Sally took the envelope and looked at it suspiciously. Then she harrumphed and went to do as I had asked.

It felt like a long time until finally, I heard footsteps on the back steps and then, ever-so-slowly—it seemed—coming down the hallway. But when Big Sally came into my room, she was alone. And she still had the envelope in her hand.

"She's not home," she said, simply. But she looked at me rather strangely, I thought, when she handed the envelope back to me. And then she left the room without another word. I must confess that I looked the envelope over very carefully, to see if it had been opened. It hadn't. But why hadn't Big Sally left it stuck in Sophie's door or something like that? Now, here I had it in my hand again, and so I was right back where I started. And all alone with it.

Why, I felt like crying, the way everything was going wrong all over the place. And also because, no matter what Ruth had ever done, it still hurt me to have to talk to her like that. So that was sitting heavy on my heart, too.

Then Big Sally came back into my room, carrying a tray with two cups of tea on it, just like it was something she did every single day of her life. She placed the tray on my dresser, handed me a cup, and without saying a single word, she took the other cup herself—and sat down in the chair by my bed.

Why, I was so surprised, you could have knocked me over with a feather.

Big Sally sitting there in one of my mama's side chairs, sipping her tea—rather noisily, I thought—and she didn't dare look me in the face. Because back then, the rules between whites and blacks were very clear-cut and strong. And not a single one of them that I could think of ever said a thing about having tea together. That's what I was thinking when she spoke—but not in that gruff voice I was so used to. This voice was soft and warm.

"Just drink your tea, Miss Anne," she said. "It'll be all right."

As if that made everything okay—that's exactly the way she said it. And the funny thing was that I took a sip of my own tea and then another, and somehow—in a way I've never been able to figure out—it was all right. Just like she said. And besides, I'd already had tea with my gardener anyway. So to hell with the rules. I certainly had a lot more than that to worry about.

When we finished, she put both cups on the tray, and only then did she look directly at me.

"I don't know what's going on here," she said, speaking very softly. "But you're a sick lady, and the doctor said I was to take good care of you. So that's what I'm gonna do. So you better start talking to me right this minute and let me see what I can do to help you."

Something about her words—or the way she said them—started me to bawling just like a little baby. All that worry and all that stress. And she came and sat down right on the side of my bed and held me in her arms and patted my back, just as if I were a little child, with my mama holding me and patting me and telling me that everything would be all right.

And I told Big Sally everything—absolutely everything.

The words ran right out of me, and I didn't leave out

a single thing. Told her about Mr. Oto being Japanese—kind of. Told her how I'd hidden him in the cabin, and how I had to take Sophie into my confidence about it, once I'd hurt my ankle.

The whole time, she just kept patting me and saying not a word, except for an "unh-huh" from time to time that arose from deep in the bottom of her chest. And when I had finished all the crying and the hiccoughing and the telling of everything there was to tell, she got me a clean handkerchief from the dresser drawer and told me to blow my nose. Then she picked up the tray and started to leave the room.

"Where are you going?" I asked her, because after all, everything was getting completely out of my control—first Sophie knew, and then Ruth started in with her terrible suspicions, and now I'd told Big Sally everything. Why, if I kept on like that, I may as well just go out in the street and holler it to everyone who would listen.

"I'm not going anywhere, right now. But I've got some thinking to do. Because I'm gonna take care of you, just like the doctor said," she replied. And that's all she would say about it. Just went on back in the kitchen and clattered the pots and pans something fierce and scrubbed some more of the flowers off my linoleum floor.

It was about thirty minutes later—seemed to me like a lifetime of lying there and wondering what she meant—when she came back to my room.

"I got it figured," she said, as if that made sense. "I

know where to find Miss Sophie. And I know what needs to be done. Just you rest now, and leave everything to me."

So she left again. And this time, she didn't need to take the note.

Chapter Twenty-nine

All Big Sally had to do was walk across the street and then cut down behind the Baptist Church and out along a sandy path until she came to the riverbank. And there Sophie was, sitting in the old canvas chair—in that strange, still heat—and gazing out at the slow-moving river.

Sophie jumped just a little when she heard Big Sally clumping toward her.

"Is Miss Anne all right?" Sophie asked, seeing how Big Sally was moving toward her at quite a rapid pace.

"She's all right—gonna be a lot better time I get done doing what needs doing." With that, Big Sally sat down on the ground right by Sophie's chair with a grunt and plucked a few sprigs of weed to twirl in her fingers before she began talking right out toward the river, as if that's what she were speaking to. As if Sophie weren't even there.

"We've all got funny things about us. Places inside us

that's specially tender—little sore spots, you might say. Take me, for instance. I know how all the ladies in this town make fun of me. How I want everything so clean. But there's a good reason for it."

She stopped and looked up at Sophie, full in the face, staring.

"I guess you don't remember me anymore," Big Sally said. "But you used to play with me. Before your mama made you stop coming." Big Sally's eyes sparkled bitterly. "Before your mama said we was dirty. You used to call me *Queen* Sally. Said it was a special name for me 'cause I was your friend."

Sophie looked at the broad, dark face—the deep, unsmiling eyes and pendulous lips. Magically, the face of Sally slowly began to emerge. Sally—her friend of a childhood that had ended so long ago. The large, liquid eyes, always somber under the straight, dark brows. The childish mouth held in a tight line, as if in imitation of a disapproving adult. And how, even when it was Sally's turn to be pushed in the tire swing, she never smiled, but kept her baleful stare on the younger children— that was the job her mama had given her, watching the younger ones—so that as she swung back and forth in long, gliding sweeps, the eyes slid back and forth, back and forth, always on the children. Large and serious eyes so misplaced in a child's face.

Sally! Queen Sally! How could I not have recognized you? Sophie was thinking, though it hadn't yet converted itself to words she could speak aloud. And thinking, too, that in one way, at least, Big Sally was the very

· 194 ·

same as she had been all those years ago. She still took it upon herself to be in charge, even though all the little brothers and sisters she'd cared for were surely grown.

"Oh, Sally!" Sophie moaned. "How I wondered about you, after your mama took you all and went to Macon! Why, I used to walk down to that little crab-house restaurant sometimes after you went away, just to remember how much I loved you!"

"Humph!" Big Sally's grunt was one of disbelief.

"I did!" Sophie protested. "I did love you! And I still do!"

Another *humph*, but softer. "You stopped coming to play. You let your mama make you stay away 'cause she said we was dirty!"

"*I* never thought you were dirty!" Sophie protested.

"Maybe not, but you stopped coming," Big Sally argued.

"I know," Sophie whispered. "I had to obey my mama. I *had* to."

"I guess I can understand that," Big Sally admitted. "I sure enough had to obey *my* mama."

"And besides," Sophie added, "it was all Miss Ruth's fault. All her fault that I lost you."

"Well, it was a long time ago," Sally said in a whisper. "A long time ago, but things are still pretty much the same around here."

"I'm so sorry!" Sophie's apology was genuine and heartfelt.

"It's okay," Big Sally said. "We can't go back and change what happened."

"But you came back—you came back to this little town. Did you come back to your mama's little house under the bridge?"

"I did that, indeed. After my mama passed on."

"Oh. I'm sad to hear that."

"Yes—but I came on back here to live 'cause all my brothers and sisters grew up and moved away, so I didn't have any family left in Macon at all. Only thing for me to do was come back to my mama's little house, where her spirit and all the spirits of my brothers and sisters still seem to be hanging around. Why, the other morning, I woke up thinking I smelled those crab cakes and hush puppies, just like my mama used to make."

Sophie smiled at the memory of those wonderful afternoons when Sally's mama would spread clean newspapers on the backyard table and bring out the steaming hot crab cakes, hush puppies, and fried fish and pile them all in the middle of the table.

"You want to know how I come to clean things so good?"

Sophie nodded.

"Make all those white ladies feel like they been living in a pigsty before. Make *them* feel dirty." And in the next breath Sally switched right over to a different topic, without so much as missing a beat. "So I know there's some kind of a good reason for what you've been doing. But it's got you in a whole heap of trouble, sure enough."

And it caught Sophie completely by surprise, for here she had been wondering how on earth she could have failed to recognize Sally, even though Sophie hadn't thought of her in a long time. Not until Miss Ruth started all that fuss about the book discussion group. And Sophie had never even thought to try and find out what had finally happened to her or where she lived. Or anything.

Through all of those thoughts, Big Sally's incomprehensible statement intruded.

"Trouble?" Sophie finally managed the word. *What on earth is she talking about?*

"Yes, *trouble*," Big Sally repeated. " 'Cause Miss Ruth's been over to Miss Anne's this afternoon, and she knows all about you going down to that old fishing cabin of Miss Anne's papa's."

"Oh, Lord!" Sophie breathed, and it was definitely more prayer than a lament.

"Sure enough! Amen to that!" Big Sally agreed.

"But how?"

"Guess she's been spying is all. That's no surprise to you, is it?"

"No, but . . ."

"No *buts* about it. You should have known somebody'd find out. This town? Thought you'd keep something a secret in *this* town?" Big Sally's sidelong gaze and slowly shaking head answered her own question. And also implied—most silently—that Sophie had been one big fool.

"What does she know, other than I've been going there?" Sophie asked. For if Miss Ruth had been spying and had followed her to the cabin, maybe she knew about Mr. Oto being there too. *Oh, Lord!*

"She doesn't know nothing else. And she won't. Miss Anne done made sure of that."

"And what do you know?" Sophie asked, for suddenly it had dawned upon her exactly what she and Big Sally were discussing.

"I know it all," Big Sally answered. "Miss Anne unloaded the whole thing on me just a little while ago."

"You know about *him?*" Because whatever Big Sally called "the whole thing" just might *not* be the whole thing. *Couldn't be,* Sophie was thinking desperately. *Because even Miss Anne doesn't know everything. What all has happened between Mr. Oto and me.*

"And now I've seen your face this afternoon, I know a lot more than Miss Anne does." Again, the voice intruded into Sophie's spinning thoughts. "So I know it won't do any good telling you not to go down there again."

"Oh, but I won't go again," Sophie said simply. Because whatever it took to keep him safe was what she would do.

"Well, that's a blessing I sure didn't expect," Big Sally sighed. Then she looked at Sophie for a long time with those deep and somber eyes. "But if you do decide to go down there, you come get me. I'll go with you. Stay outside and make sure that old busybody don't come near the cabin."

As she spoke, Big Sally obviously felt an immediate pleasure toward the vague idea of waylaying Miss Ruth on a dark path by the river. And the thought must have occurred to Sophie, too. So that in the midst of that deadly seriousness, Sophie and Big Sally looked at each other for a long, silent moment before Big Sally's eyebrows shot up into the very edge of her hair and she started speaking suddenly and with an animation that Sophie could never have imagined.

Her voice fell to a deep and vicious whisper. "Dark as midnight down there. Me standing there in that deep, old dark. Me! Big as a mountain! Black as the night! So can't nobody see a thing! And along she'll come, snooping and sniffing, just like a old dog after hisself a girlfriend!" Here, she scrunched her shoulders, wrinkled her nose as if at some unpleasant odor, and moved her head from side to side—sniffing and sniffing.

Sophie watched and listened almost in disbelief— wondering at the same time how Big Sally—Queen Sally—could make herself look almost exactly like that dried-up little Miss Ruth.

"*Jump* out at her!" Sally's sudden voice booming and the great arms thrown wide. "Me! Bigger'n her by a hundred, a *thousand* times! Jump right on her! Throw her down on the ground! Yank them ugly pink bloomers off her ugly old white ass! Wrap 'em 'round her head like the rag my mama had to make me wear wrapped 'round my head and then hook her up high on a big tree limb and leave her like that, squealing and hollering and flapping around just like a old scarecrow! Leave her there forever and ever! *Amen!*"

Sophie was coming closer and closer to doing something like clapping her hands, but she didn't know if it was because of Big Sally's vivid description and wild gesticulations or because the mere idea of anyone's doing such a thing to Miss Ruth filled her with a surprising sense of delight.

And maybe that's why—when Big Sally shouted "Amen!"—Sophie shouted *"Amen!"* right after her, her own voice startling her. And it certainly startled Big Sally, too. For one long moment, she gazed incredulously at Sophie. Because it was the very first time in Sally's whole life that she had found *anything* to be amusing.

So that the corners of the big mouth moved upward, involuntarily, higher and higher until they finally succeeded in lifting the large, heavy upper lip. The edges of straight, gleaming teeth appeared, and the teeth grew larger and larger, until the entire bottom half of her face seemed to have been replaced by a huge, expansive, dazzling smile.

"Hallelujah!" Big Sally shouted, lifting her grin toward heaven and bringing up her hands so that the white palms looked as if they were waiting for the Great God Almighty Himself to drop something into them.

"Yes! Hallelujah!" echoed Sophie.

"It's so *good!*" Big Sally yelled.

"Yes, it is! It's good!" Sophie repeated after her.

"You got to have bad feelings toward some folks!" Sally yelled. " 'Cause they do things that's bad!"

"They sure do!"

"And you got to have good feelings about other folks!" Big Sally yelled. " 'Cause they deserve good feelings. They deserve to be loved!"

"Yes, they do!" Sophie answered.

But by now, she was so caught up in the whole thing that she didn't even know what the words meant. That is, not until she realized that Sally had fallen silent and was gazing at her with big, luminous eyes that were so deep and so kind, Sophie felt she could fall right into them and drown in complete happiness. Having someone look at her like that. With love. The way Mr. Oto looked at her, but different. But still love.

"What?" Sophie asked her finally, after they had gazed at each other silently for a long time, each caught up in her own thoughts.

"You hear what you said?" Big Sally's voice was soft.

"What?" Sophie repeated, senselessly.

"That some folks deserve to be loved."

"I said that?"

"You sure did. And you're one of them."

"What do you mean?" Suddenly, Sophie felt close to tears. But she didn't know why. Maybe it had something to do with all the praising and the hollering she'd done. *Mama always said that kind of thing can get people all stirred up so they don't know what they're doing or saying anymore.*

"Means it was good for you to love Henry," Big Sally said simply. "And it would have been even better if he'd loved you back." Sophie drew a sharp breath, but Big Sally pretended not to notice. She simply went on: "And now it's good for you to let somebody else love you, now Henry's gone. Been gone. And if somebody loves you, it don't matter where he came from or what he looks like. Or nothing."

But Sophie was wondering what on earth Sally was saying. How did she know about Henry? But more importantly, how did she know about Mr. Oto? His feelings for her? And her own feelings for him? Did Miss Anne know about this and tell her?

"How did you know?" Sophie asked in a very serious—almost accusatory—tone. "Miss Anne didn't tell you." Sophie didn't realize how emphatically she knew that, until she heard the conviction in her own voice.

"No. Miss Anne never said such a thing, And she sure don't know about it, else she would have told me." Big Sally answered. "I'm the one figured it out. Didn't take much, though. 'Cause I know that look on your face."

"Look?"

"I saw it the first time you looked at me after your mama made you quit coming to play. Then, years later, when my mama brought us back for a weekend, I saw you one day when Henry was coming down the street, and you all spoke in passing. That's all it was. But I saw your face. Saw it, too, when we all found out he wasn't coming home from the war. This time, I want to see that in your face for somebody you can have."

"But he's going to be gone, too," Sophie said, and a deep and lasting sigh followed her words like a door closing.

"No." Big Sally said the word with the finality of someone who has absolutely no doubt. "He won't go without you. Not if you go with him."

To that, Sophie had no response. She was remembering how fully she had expected the great crane to step out of the bushes. And if he had, she would have gone back to the cabin. Gone away with him.

But where? Sophie was thinking. *In this whole, wide world, where is the place we could go? No. War robbed me before, and war will rob me again.*

"I wish you could see your face," Big Sally's voice broke through Sophie's thinking. "Look just like a dead bird."

Yes, Sophie thought. *Those poor, eyeless little things.* And Sophie's own voice out of her childhood: *Why do you keep them, Mama?*

Because nothing lasts, Sophie. One minute they're pretty and alive and flying from tree to tree. Next minute, they're stiff and cold on the ground.

"Well, you think on it," Big Sally said at last. "And if you decide to go down there to him tonight, you come get me. Knock on that little back window. I'll hear you."

"Yes," Sophie answered. "You'll hear me."

"But let me tell you this: If you go down there tonight, you're not to come back. You go on and go away with him. You hear me?"

"I hear you."

"So you either go or you stay. One or the other."

"Yes."

Big Sally stood, silently, looking at Sophie. Stood there for so long that finally, Sophie looked at her, expectantly. And then Big Sally spoke with great deliberation and also with kindness.

"I didn't never see Henry look at you the way you looked at him."

It was the last thing Big Sally said to her old friend. Only her clumping footsteps in the grass and then silence.

It took that long for Sophie to hear exactly what Big Sally had said.

He did! Sophie was tempted to yell into the emptiness Big Sally left behind her, but something stopped the words.

He did *love me!*

Very clearly and right before her eyes, Henry's smile floated in the moisture-laden air. But something tight in her throat. Lodged there, deeply entrenched and completely immovable.

He loved me! The silent words fluttered weakly against the back of her eyes and then were still. Blessedly still.

Sophie, sitting on the riverbank, where she had always taken the grief, to mix it with solitude. Grief for the lost love who had existed, at first, like a tiny pinpoint of faraway light. Light that would never have begun glowing at all, had Henry come home from the war. Because then, it would have been the gaze of his eyes that always looked slightly beyond her. The polite smile whose roots never reached his heart.

But when he was lost, that sad, sweet light began to grow, fueled by her own deepest dreams. Until, at last, the glowing image of her imaginary lover had stood in her full sunshine. And had stayed there, young and beautiful and alive and in love with her. For over thirty years.

A thing to keep forever. Like sad little mummy-birds in a box on the pantry shelf.

Dear Lord!

Chapter Thirty

*M*iss Anne said:

When Big Sally came back, she came right into my room and sat down on the side of my bed.

"It's all taken care of. You don't need to worry about it," she said.

"But taken care of, how?" I asked, because I was really used to knowing what was going on. Certainly, I trusted Big Sally—I'd better trust her, what with the secret I'd blubbered out to her. But I still wanted to know.

But she just looked at me and smiled. Why, I'd never seen her smile before in her whole life. Never even heard of such a thing. Her smiling.

Looked just like a big old sphinx, she did.

Chapter Thirty-one

For hours, Mr. Oto stayed under the cot, just as silent as a ghost. No longer out of fear—for his heart had stopped its frantic thudding when he knew that Miss Ruth was looking at his painting of Sophie as the Crane-Wife. Loathing, then, had replaced his initial fear. And grief. So that, even after she was gone for a long time, he was immobilized by the most incredible exhaustion he had ever felt. Too tired, almost, to wonder if she would figure everything out about him.

When, finally, he felt some semblance of his strength returning, he came out from under the cot and the first thing he did was to look at the painting. Look at Sophie sitting in the chair, with the sunlight on her pale arms and the hat shading her face. The loose tendrils of hair by her cheek. Behind her, the distinctly sensual figure of the great crane, with the wing-feathers somehow one with her arms. The great, purple eyes filled with passion.

But what he also saw in the painting—that which no one else would be able to see—was Sophie's mind focused on that particular sky over where the ocean and the river came together. The place of no edges. Of oneness. Of infinity.

He kneeled down on the floor before the painting, sat back on his heels, and continued to gaze at it—meditating over it—for the whole remainder of the long afternoon. Because in the moment he saw it again, he resolved that he would look at it as long as he pleased. That he would not move. Not hide. No matter who came—even if it was Miss Ruth. He would not move.

He never stirred until the long, slanted fingers of sunlight came beneath the bottom of the torn blanket over the window. The wind rising—he could tell from the whisperings of it in the tall Australian pines. And an aroma in the breeze that crept around the edges of the blanket. The aroma of moisture and warm, Gulf air. A storm, perhaps.

Finally then, he stood and bowed deeply to the painting once again before he began moving quietly and deliberately about the cabin—gathering and folding the sheets from the cot, removing the towel from where it hung on a nail near the door, taking the remaining cans of food and the last bottle of water, and carrying everything out into the back of the cabin. Into the deepness of dusk beneath the great trees. There, he dug a large hole with his hands in the soft, sandy soil and placed those things in it. And covered them up most carefully, being sure to brush a little pine straw and a few bits of dried grass over the place where he had dug.

The cabin now was a vacant stage—where the happiest hours of his long life had played themselves out. The painting, alone, remained, still resting on the wooden box against the wall.

He took it into his hands with great reverence and slowly rolled one side of it inward until the painting was no longer a painting, but a cylinder of white paper. This, he tucked carefully into his belt and then looked around the cabin once more before he lifted the blanket for the last time, went out into the yard, and walked off toward the ocean through the ever-deepening dusk.

By the time he was close to the shore, the darkness was complete and the wind had begun whipping in hot, moist gusts that fluttered his trouser legs and shirt-sleeves. As he came up over the last sand dune, the wind drove the sharp and stinging sand right into his face, so that he found himself squinting painfully at an entirely different ocean from the one where he and Sophie had been together, the night before.

For in place of that dark expanse of rolling water glistening in the moonlight, this ocean was glowing with ghostly froth—like a wild, living thing that was trying to escape from its confines. Yesterday's long, easy waves that lifted slowly to curl over into creamy froth upon the sand were replaced by choppy, black wavelets whose foaming tops were shaved off by the wind and hurled through the air.

Leaning against the wind, he walked across the short

expanse of beach and into the churning water, where he removed the rolled painting from his belt.

"I give to you, my Crane-Wife, the great dream of your spirit. I return you to the ocean and the river. No one will ever gaze upon you with irreverence, and I will love you forever."

He lowered the painting into the black, churning water, and held it under while the waves battered against his knees and splashed salt water into his eyes—holding it until he felt the paper growing heavy in his hands, absorbing the ocean water. The current lifted it from his loosened fingers and pulled it away. It reappeared briefly in the uppermost portion of yet another angry wave, sodden and undulating like a flounder, while the strong undertow tugged at his knees.

How easy it would be, he thought. *To have the ocean take me also, here and now. Only a kneeling would do it.*

But his knees did not bend. Because giving a painting to the ocean was easy. For the frothing waves would lift away the paint. So that if ever the paper washed upon some shore, it would be just that—paper. Not a painting.

But if he gave himself to that same ocean, and if his body later came ashore, he would still be recognized. Even in death, he would still incriminate Miss Anne. And Sophie. So he did not kneel.

My dear Sophie! If only you could have come to me on this night, I would never have let you go again.

Sophie went straight home from the riverfront soon after Big Sally left, and when she was once more back in her own bedroom, she shed her clothes, glanced briefly in the mirror at herself, slipped on a cool, cotton wrapper and sat down at the dresser to decide exactly how to do what was to be done.

Beside her brush was the completely withered sprig of bougainvillea. She picked it up and studied it, turning the stem in her fingers until the movement of the sprig, reflected in the mirror, caught her eye.

She gazed at herself, as if her image would speak to her in silence. Say whatever it was she needed to hear. But the moment she saw her own face, she realized that what was gazing back at her was someone she hadn't known before. Her face, but no longer familiar.

No longer grieving for . . . what? . . . Henry? Her own youth? The lost years?

No. This face bore no trace of sadness and very little of age, in fact. This face was vital and alive and with the heightened color of round cheeks glowing between deep green eyes and the white V of her skin at the neckline of the blue wrapper.

The slow, silent dance of the faded bougainvillea in the mirror, and watching in strange detachment as her hand came up slowly toward the neckline of the wrapper and hesitated only briefly before slipping it from the rounded shoulders. So that her pale body was, at last, revealed to her in the glass.

The breasts somewhat pendulous, and the neck slightly lined. But the face more alive and vibrant than it had ever been, even in her youth. The eyes smoldering with something unknown. She raised her arms, then crossed them behind her head, and gazed at herself for a very long time. Until her image lost its meaning, fragmented into a meaningless montage of brows and mouth and breasts and arms.

And it was taking very little for her to see the delicate feathers and the purple eyes of the great crane, right there in her mirror.

And what is it that happens between a man and a woman? she wondered. *What secret things will I learn from loving a man who is real?*

When the dusk was deepening rapidly and the wind steadily rising, she finished packing the small suitcase— even though she knew that she would wait for full dark before she left. As soon as she had closed the lid and snapped it shut, there was only one thing left for her to do before she would be free, at last. She went straight to the pantry, to where the familiar box sat alone on the bottom shelf, and she didn't need to lift the lid to see the eyeless, mummified feather-creatures inside.

Silently, she carried the box—as light as if it were empty—out onto the back porch, where the increasing wind flung open the screen door, as if holding it open for her to pass through. Out into the yard to where the wind was blowing wildly—wind that ripped off the box lid, just as she tossed the mummified bodies into the air—wind that swept them away, as if they still could fly.

And at that very moment, there was a sudden flurry of live wings in the twilight backyard, where a flock of mourning doves lifted in one enormous and swift movement out of the swaying crepe myrtle tree, strong, white wings bearing them straight up and into the last light.

Beneath the sudden whirring of their wings, Sophie stood and watched where spirit-children shrieked and chased each other and took turns in the tire swing, laughing and pushing each other higher and higher into the twilight sky.

Grove! Wait for me! I'm coming!

In the small room behind Miss Anne's kitchen, Big Sally had gone to bed early. Lying awake and listening to the whine of the rising wind, she was startled a little when she heard the fronds of a cabbage-palm near her window flap-flapping against the glass.

Sophie?

No.

No one there.

Finally, in spite of the wind and the intermittent flapping of the palm fronds on the window, Big Sally felt herself drifting into that half-world between sleeping and waking.

Where she was a child again, wearing the red rag wrapped around her head. And Mama said, "You take good care of the little ones, Sally. You hear?"

"Yessm, Mama."

And little Sophie there, too, in her dream. In a white pinafore, darting around the yard, laughing and squealing. The bright green eyes and the white arms. Like a little white egret.

It was Sophie's turn to swing in the tire swing and Sally's turn to push her. Higher and higher, up against the blue sky and the green leaves.

Fly, little white bird! Fly!

And the white wings reaching for the blue air and the strong downbeat flapping against the red rag wrapped around Sally's head.

Flap-flap!

TAP-TAP.

Chapter Thirty-two

*M*iss Anne said:

Big Sally went to bed early that night, but before she did, she brought me a cup of tea and my book and plumped up my pillows and smoothed my sheets. I thought of asking her once again to tell me how she'd "taken care of things," but something about the broadness of her shoulders stopped the words before I could utter them.

And after all, I really didn't have to ask. Quite obviously, she'd found Sophie, admonished her not to go to the cabin again, and explained to her about Ruth's snooping.

Nothing so complicated about that. So I said good night to Sally, drank my tea, and then read myself to sleep.

I don't know how long I'd been asleep when that old devil wind waked me. It was blowing so hard that it shook the whole house, and the curtains at my window whipped and fluttered out into the room like ghosts.

"*Sally?*" I called out. No answer. But with all that wind blowing like that, it would be hard for her to hear me, all the way in that little room behind the kitchen. And so I pulled the sheet up over my head and listened to the wind. A hurricane. It had to be a hurricane.

In only an hour or so the wind had gotten much worse, and I heard the back door bang open and slam hard against the wall. Scared me to death, it did. I reached over to turn on the lamp, but the electricity was out, and the house just as black as that wild black night outside.

"Sally?" I yelled into the darkness. "See to the back door, will you? Wind's blown it open!"

"It's me, Miss Anne." A man's voice from the hallway. "Sheriff."

What on earth?

A flashlight beam snaking along the hallway and the sound of shuffling feet. A grunting sound in the darkness and then the beam of light coming into my room and behind it, the big figure of the sheriff and him wearing a black rain slicker and puddling water all over my floor.

"Don't be alarmed, Miss Anne," he said. "We found Big Sally out on the edge of town, and she's got a broken arm and a cut on her head. Must have gotten hit by a falling branch or something. Me and the doctor are going to put her to bed, and I'll come back in a few minutes with somebody to take care of you all."

Big Sally? Out in this storm? But why?

"What on earth was she doing outside in this?" I

asked, but the sheriff was already heading back out my bedroom door.

"Don't know. Maybe trying to see if her mama's old house down by the bridge was okay," he said over his shoulder. "But right now I got folks down there still, needing help. It's awful bad."

"It's a hurricane?" I asked.

"Yessm, it's a hurricane, all right."

And with that, he was gone, leaving me all alone and knowing that Big Sally was hurt and in the bed in my back room and me not even able to get to her to help her. Or to find out why she'd gone out in such a terrible storm.

So I had to lie there just like a stick and listen to all that wind buffeting the house and wonder about it all. Lots of trouble down at the end of town, the sheriff had said.

And what about my papa's cabin, farther out? Was that where she'd gone? To find Mr. Oto and take him somewhere else to hide him? Because of Ruth?

About thirty minutes passed—seemed like much longer, of course, with me lying there in the dark, just as helpless as a baby.

Then I heard the back door opening again and slamming back and hitting the wall hard. Heavy footsteps coming back down the hall.

"Miss Anne?" the sheriff called to me. "It's me again. I've brought somebody to help take care of you . . . and Sally."

And no sooner were the words out of his mouth

than—of all things—Ruth's mean face peered around my door. Her just as mad as a wet hen and with rainwater dripping out of her hair.

"The very idea of such a thing!" she hissed at me. "Why, he practically kidnapped me! Make me take care of a colored woman, will he? Well, we'll see about that!"

Oh, Lord.

Well, life sure hands us some unexpected things, sure enough. Like that hurricane so very late in the year. And Ruth having to play nursemaid to me . . . and to Big Sally. Well, I tell you, I was mighty glad that I had to stay in bed in my own room, because there were sure going to be plenty of sparks flying around the rest of my house that night. Until the storm would be over and then I expected Eulalie would come and take over for Ruth.

Because it was common knowledge that Eulalie was terrified of hurricanes, and whenever one came, she took right to her bed and stayed there until it was past. Wouldn't come out for anything. But I sure wished that weren't so. Because there couldn't have been anyone worse for the job than Ruth. It just made everything more miserable than it already was.

At first, of course, I was just intent on seeing if my house would hold up in the wind. But Ruth was plenty mad, as I'd expected she would be. Said the sheriff had *shanghaied* her—that's what she called it—and there was just no settling her down. Why, she made more noise than the hurricane!

"I'll take care of *you*," she yelled above the howling wind. "Even if you did insult me and hurt me right to the quick! But Doc is one big fool if he thinks I'm going to take care of . . . colored!" Ruth waggled her head toward the back of the house, where Big Sally was.

"Ruth, she's a human being and needs taking care of," I yelled back. "Besides—I've listened to you talking and talking for your whole life about what you call Christian charity—now I want you to show it to me!"

"Some one *you* are," she sputtered back at me. "To talk about Christian anything—you haven't been to church in a month of Sundays!"

Well, I knew then that there was no getting it across to Ruth that being in church every Sunday and being a good Christian didn't necessarily mean one and the same thing. And I was vexed with her. I had plenty to worry about, without trying to persuade her to take care of Big Sally.

"I'll take care of her myself," I yelled, tossing back the sheet and trying to swing my feet to the floor. But Ruth saw my swollen and discolored leg above the ankle that was encased in plaster, and she relented.

"No. I'll do it—but on one condition."

"What's that?" I asked wearily. I might have known she'd drive a bargain. A hard one. But she had to take care of Big Sally, because there was no one else to do it. And besides, she hadn't said another thing to me about the cabin, and I guess I was grateful for that.

"I'll wait on Big Sally . . ." She shuddered a little, in revulsion. "And you'll come to church."

I hesitated only a moment before I agreed. Because I had something in mind that I was sure going to enjoy.

"It's a deal!" I yelled back at her. And I think she was more than a little surprised, although she did a good job of covering it up. After all, she was the one who had suggested it. And of course, she kept her word.

Soon afterward, she took a tray in to Big Sally in the back bedroom, but she slammed the tray down so hard on the dresser back there that I could hear the dishes rattling all the way in my room, even over the sound of the wind.

And Big Sally laughing hard enough to rattle all the hinges on the doors.

Me alone in my room, listening to the two of them and wondering what was happening to Mr. Oto. And why Big Sally had been so far down at the other end of town in that terrible storm. And where on earth Mr. Oto really was.

That was certainly a long, long night, but when it was over, the storm went away with the darkness. And just as I expected, Eulalie came just as soon as the wind had stopped and took over from Ruth, who left right away—but only after she stuck her head into my room and said, "You needn't worry yourself about your . . . friend . . . back there." Again, she waggled her head toward the back room. "Strong as a bull. Mean as a snake. And I'll never forgive you, Anne. Making me wait on her. Just like a servant! So don't you forget your part of the bargain!" And with that, Ruth was gone, at last.

And it was ever so much better, having Eulalie there, because I knew she would be just as tender and loving with Big Sally as she had been with all her stray cats. And with Mr. Oto. And with anyone who needed help— black or white.

One thing, though—I asked Eulalie right away if she'd please go see if my papa's old fishing cabin was still there. Said it lightly, so it would seem that I was merely interested in knowing whether it survived the storm. Because if the cabin was still there and if Mr. Oto was still in it, if Eulalie saw him—then I could let her in on the secret about our hiding him. Eulalie would have understood. Whether she could have kept her mouth shut about it was something else, but I had to risk it.

But she said right off that there was no need for her to go down there at all. That everything from that end of town and on down the coast was gone. Or so the sheriff said. And after all, Eulalie reminded me, it was just an old shack, so I shouldn't worry myself about it. And with that, she went right back to the kitchen, from which the most wonderful aromas were wafting down the hallway. But when she brought a tray into my room—and it laden with fried chicken and mashed potatoes and English peas and fresh, buttered biscuits— I couldn't eat a bite.

All I could do was wonder about Mr. Oto. And was he all right?

Oh, it was terrible.

When Eulalie came back in for the tray, she never fussed at me the least little bit, but she looked at all the untouched food still there with real grief in her eyes. And I guess she thought she had figured out what was wrong with me, because in a little while, she brought Big Sally—leaning on her quite hard—down the hallway and helped her to sit down in the chair next to my bed.

"I figured you all needed a little visit together," Eulalie said. "Doc said it was okay." And she went out of the room, smiling and looking back at us, firmly convinced that I was just a little bit lonely and that bringing Big Sally to "visit" with me would solve everything. How I wished that were true!

Of course, I was certainly glad to see Big Sally—certainly had a lot of questions for her. One of her arms was in a cast and a sling, and she had a plaster bandage over her left eyebrow. But otherwise, she looked just as big and strong as she ever was. I waited until Eulalie closed the door all the way before I dared to speak.

"What were you doing out in that storm?" I whispered right away.

But the doctor must have had Big Sally on some kind of strong pain medicine, because her eyes were funny-looking—with the pupils gone all wide. Either that, or getting hit on the head like that had hurt her more than it looked like on the surface. That little plaster bandage.

"Doing?" she asked, most sincerely, as if it were a word she had never heard before.

"Yes—what were you doing out in that storm? Did you go to the cabin?"

"Sheriff found me," she said.

"Yes. I know all about that, but what were you doing out in it? Where were you going?"

But Big Sally just blinked at me, as if she didn't understand a thing I was saying.

"You went out in that storm," I said. "But why? Sheriff said you may have gone to see if your mama's old house was all right."

"That's it," she said happily.

"That was it?" I pressed.

"What was it?" Big Sally asked, drawing her eyebrows together and crinkling the plaster patch.

"Listen to me," I pleaded with her, and I felt close to tears. "Did you go down to the cabin?"

She just looked at me, and her face was as blank as a baby's. "Cabin?"

Dear Lord!

Clearly, she wasn't able to answer my questions. She'd forgotten everything about Mr. Oto hiding in my papa's old cabin. And I still didn't know what had happened to him. My throat got so tight, I could hardly breathe. And I couldn't tell whether I was going to cry harder than I'd ever cried in my life or whether I was going to leap out of bed—broken ankle and all—and grab her and choke the answer out of her!

"I do better than you," Big Sally said, right out of the blue. And she sure didn't look so blank anymore.

"Better than me?"

"Better than you at not saying things that shouldn't be said," she replied. "But you listen to me—and you listen real good, because I'm only going to say this once: Don't you worry about anything. I took care of it all."

I certainly did search her face, then. What was she trying to tell me, without telling me?

And could I trust that she even knew what she was saying? Because of her being so confused?

"And another thing . . ." A strange smile was on her face, and I was remembering how I could hear her laughing at Ruth all the way in my room and in spite of that howling wind. "From now on, my name is *Queen* Sally."

I wondered if she was completely out of her mind. And how could I believe a thing she said?

While I was sitting there, studying her face and trying to decide, she closed her eyes and fell asleep. So that all I could hear was her snoring. And that made about as much sense as anything else that had come out of her mouth.

A little while later, Eulalie came back. "I hope you all had a nice little visit," she said, and waked Big Sally by touching that massive shoulder so gently and then led her back down the hallway, just like a sleepy little child.

I fretted myself for most of the afternoon, but when Eulalie brought me a cold chicken sandwich a little later, she delivered it with such hopefulness in her face that I made myself eat it. And after that, I felt a little better. And finally, I decided that even if Big Sally seemed to be quite confused, there could be an element of truth in what she said.

Because that's what I wanted very much to believe.

But I didn't get a chance to feel better for very long. Because things weren't through happening yet. Things that would almost break my heart.

Late that afternoon, somebody or other came up on the porch, and Eulalie went out and talked with them. I couldn't hear what they said, just low voices. I thought it was the sheriff. Probably just checking on all of us. Making sure we had everything we needed.

Eulalie didn't come back into my room until she brought my supper tray to me—a nice cup of tea and homemade soup and a plate of cookies. But the minute I saw her face, I knew that something was very, very wrong.

"What's the matter?" I asked her—because she was all red-eyed and puffy-faced. Looked even worse than she had when the doctor took Mr. Oto away from her and brought him to live in my gardener's cottage.

She looked at me for so long that I thought she'd never speak, and my mind was just racing around, trying to figure out what it was she had to tell me. Mr. Oto? Had someone found him? Alive? Or . . .

"Sophie's gone," she whispered, and her voice almost broke, what with just trying to get the words out. Why, that was the last thing I would have thought of.

"Gone?" I croaked. "Gone where?"

"Just gone," Eulalie repeated. "In the storm."

"What do you mean—gone?" Because on the one hand, it didn't make a bit of sense, whatever it was she was saying. Or trying to say. And on the other hand, I felt like someone had just kicked me right in the stomach.

"Her house is empty. No one can find her. She's gone."

Sophie!

I didn't even realize the doctor had come in the door behind Eulalie. And I also didn't realize that that horrible moaning I could hear was *me*. Not until I saw the doctor rolling up my sleeve and Eulalie holding my arm still, so he could slip the needle full of blessed oblivion into my vein.

I don't know how long I slept—if slept is the right word. And awakening wasn't like any awakening I'd ever done. Occasionally, I could see the dresser in my room or Eulalie's anxious face. Sometimes it was daylight and sometimes it was dark. Without rhyme or reason.

But at some point—I don't know when—I fluttered to wakefulness during the night and I saw Big Sally's face very close to mine.

"Big Sally?" Again, my voice was little more than a faint croak.

"You hush up that hollering you been doing! I told you not to worry! And you didn't listen to me! You're not to worry about either one of them. And I *told* you to call me *Queen* Sally! Didn't I tell you that?"

"What do you know about Sophie?" I tried to yell. "And who in the hell is *Queen* Sally?" But then I remembered how she had been hit awfully hard in the head. Still, if she knew anything, she had to tell me. She just had to. And she had to be specific.

But she wouldn't say anything else. Just glared at me. And then her face disappeared. Later, I thought that

· 226 ·

maybe I had dreamed it, gotten my hopes up for nothing. Because of my being sick and because of all that medicine Big Sally was taking. And her getting hit in the head so hard.

So I was never sure. Never.

Oh, the sheriff formed up search parties, and they all looked and looked for the longest kind of time. But they never found a thing. Not Sophie. Not Mr. Oto.

And finally, in the long run, perhaps Sophie's mama was right. Because nothing lasts.

Not even grief. Not even pain. And not even *not knowing*.

Because time heals up everything. Sooner or later.

It helped that I always held on to a lot of hope about what happened to Sophie. Thought that poor old Ruth had been right after all. Maybe Sophie just finally up and ran off at last, like we all thought she'd do when she was young and right pretty.

And yes, I certainly did keep my part of the bargain with Ruth. The very first Sunday my ankle was healed, I went to church. Took Big Sally—Queen Sally—with me, just like I'd planned on doing all along. And when we walked in together and sat down together, I wish you could have seen Ruth's face—guess she couldn't understand that Sally and I had become very, very good friends. But most of the other folks got used to it, eventually, and the two of us went to church together—at Ruth's church—every single Sunday for many, many years.

That was a new thing for me to do, go to church. But that terrible little hurricane changed a lot of things for all of us. Probably the most of all for Mr. Oto and Sophie.

So that when it was over, there was a lot more gone than just the four houses all from the far end of town. Sophie was gone, too. And Mr. Oto. And a lot of things I used to worry about that weren't worth a hill of beans anyway.

Sally's mama's old house was just fine, like most of the older houses. They all stood the blow. But part of the roof was blown away on my sunroom, that's all. And the funny thing was, that fragile little birdhouse hanging from the crepe myrtle tree beside my porch was still there when the storm was over. Can you imagine?

Tree limbs blew down all over the place, but that little birdhouse was still there. The limbs crushed most of the flowers in the garden. Knocked down all but one of the little pink dogwoods Mr. Oto planted for me. Later on, I got to where I liked it that way. It looked real pretty like that.

Eventually, I did start calling Big Sally *Queen* Sally, just like she wanted—like she insisted on—and she was surely a different person, so I guess she deserved a different name. Why, for the rest of her life, she was the sweetest, best-natured lady you would ever hope to meet. A little confused, sometimes, because she never did fully recover from that blow on her head.

I asked her to move in with me. Not as a servant, but as a friend, and she did. She's still with me, and we've sure had some good times together—besides going to church. We play cards and sit on the porch in the afternoons, and we take care of each other, too.

The only thing we've never really shared is whatever the whole story was about Mr. Oto and Sophie—not in so many words. And I don't even know if Queen Sally ever really knew what happened. Or whether she made it all up. Or whether I dreamed it.

Now that she's getting on in years, she falls asleep in her chair almost every afternoon, and she says things in her sleep—mostly, "You should have seen their eyes!"

That's a comfort to me, it is. But of course, we never know how it's going to be for us when we get older.

Or maybe it's even like she said—that she is a lot better at keeping secrets than I was.

Because I want with all my heart to believe that Sophie went off with Mr. Oto and that they are together still, so that's finally what I have come to accept as the truth. Completely.

But I never did know for sure.

So I tell the story of Sophie and Mr. Oto to anybody who'll listen—makes it seem to me like they're still here. And sometimes—when I've just told their story again and have them especially on my mind—I catch Queen Sally watching me. Just like an old hawk, I tell you! Why, she'll study me hard for a long time and then nod her head, just once. She's got that big old secret in her and won't ever let it out—not in words, that is. But I like it when she nods at me like that. And once in a long while, I think about Sophie and Mr. Oto so much that I can almost see them. Sophie just a little girl in a white dress, skipping along so happy-like. And Mr. Oto? Well, sometimes I see his face the way it always looked when something especially beautiful bloomed under his gentle care.

Then I can see them together. Sophie all grown—soft and pretty and with a lovely glow about her. And him bowing deeply to her, cherishing her with all his heart, and nurturing her into the beautiful flower she was always meant to be.

Oh! How lovely!

CC 24|2|06